When Lissa arrived at the Pine Barrens, she wanted to go straight back to Brooklyn. Even though she knew her mom, Barbara, wanted to make pottery and her dad, Nils, wanted to write, she couldn't understand why they had to be stuck in an isolated cabin in the South Jersey woods. They were always moving. Every time she began to feel settled someplace it was time to pack. Besides, she missed her friend Marcy

She hadn't known Mrs. G. or Jess then. If she had, she wouldn't have felt that way. Mrs. G. was one of the most interesting people in the world—she had probably read just about every book ever written . . . and Jess, well, she had never met a boy like him before.

Between Jess and Mrs. G., Lissa would come to really understand and love those scary woods. Maybe the Pine Barrens wouldn't be just another stopping place after all.

The Stopping Place

BY MARDEN DAHLSTEDT

Drawings by Allen Davis

G.P. Putnam's Sons   New York

J
Dah
c. 1

The author would like to thank the *Today*
magazine of the Philadelphia *Inquirer* for
permission to reprint the song lyrics
which appear on pages 78 and 79.

Library of Congress Cataloging in Publication Data

Dahlstedt, Marden. The Stopping Place
[1. Friendship—Fiction. 2. Forest Fires—
Fiction. 3. New Jersey—Fiction]
I. Davis, Allen. II. Title
PZ7.D1517St3   [Fic]   75-43616
ISBN 0-399-20496-2
ISBN 0-399-60986-5

PRINTED IN THE UNITED STATES OF AMERICA

Designed by Aileen Friedman

In loving memory of my parents,
Glenn and Lillian Armstrong,
and of
Helen Murphy Ochsenhirt

The
Stopping
Place

JUNE

1

"I just knew it would be a rotten day," Lissa remarked gloomily.

Rain drummed on the roof of the U-Haul truck, and its windshield wipers cut lopsided blurry arcs on the glass. On both sides of the Garden State Parkway pine trees loomed, webbed with fog.

Nils, Lissa's father, gripped the steering wheel tighter and strained to see through the downpour.

"Watch for signs, will you, and we'll pull into the next service area. I could use a cup of coffee."

He glanced into the rear-view mirror.

"Barbara's still with us," he said cheerfully.

Lissa's mother was following the truck in their old red VW, piled high with last-minute leftovers of their moving.

"There's a sign," Lissa cried. "Two miles to the next stop."

Nils checked his watch.

"It's only ten—we're making pretty good time. We ought to be there around noon."

He flicked on the turn signal and in a few minutes pulled the truck to a stop in front of the highway restaurant.

"Run for it, *min elskling*."

Nils always called her *min elskling*. In Norwegian it meant "my darling."

Lissa clicked open the door of the truck cab, jumped to the ground, and landed squarely in the middle of a deep puddle. Chilly water soaked through her tennis shoes. She dashed for the shelter of the swinging doors.

In a minute Nils and Barbara joined her, laughing and brushing raindrops from their hair.

"My feet are soaked," Lissa grumbled.

"I just heard a weather report on the car radio," Barbara told her. "Clearing by this afternoon."

"How's Dewey?"

"That dog could sleep through an earthquake." Barbara laughed. "He's snoring on the back seat beside the rubber plant."

They slid onto stools at the counter and gave the waitress their orders.

"Hey! Hey! We're really on our way!"

Nils slapped his great hands flat on the counter, startling an old couple sitting beside them. Lissa felt a twinge of embarrassment. She glanced at her father, a huge man in his faded blue work shirt, jeans, and scuffed boots. He had a flaming mane of red hair and a bushy beard. Lissa adored Nils, but sometimes she wished he weren't so . . . well, *conspicuous*.

"By golly, tonight we'll be sleeping in the woods!" he crowed.

Barbara stirred the coffee that had been placed in front of her and looked anxiously at her daughter.

"You're going to love the cabin, Lissa," she said softly. "It's so quiet and peaceful and . . ."

Her voice trailed off.

"Yah! A whole new better way of life!"

Nils never seemed to just talk. He shouted. His heavy Norwegian accent didn't help either. Heads were turning to stare at them.

"I have to go to the rest room," Lissa mumbled. "I'll be right back."

As she stood by the sink a few minutes later, dribbling grainy soap powder into her wet hands, Lissa stared at herself in the mirror. A tall surly-looking stranger stared back, long, straight wheat-colored hair and sea-blue eyes with the life gone out of them.

I'm Lissa Evorssen, she thought in sudden panic.

What am I doing here?

I don't want to be here at all! I don't want to be on my way to some godforsaken cabin in the South Jersey woods. I want to be back in Brooklyn, meeting Marcy for lunch at the Pizza Hut.

No! I just won't think about Marcy now.

Barbara stuck her head in the washroom door.

"Come on, Lissa—we're leaving."

For the next hour Nils sang at the top of his lungs. His repertoire was endless, and he sang Norwegian folk songs, scraps from opera, a Schumann lullaby, and some Bob Dylan.

"Come on," he urged Lissa, during one pause for breath. "Sing!"

"I have a lousy voice."

"Nonsense! Every Norwegian can sing."

"I'm only part Norwegian."

"Yah, but you got all the best parts!"

Shortly before noon they turned off the parkway at the New Gretna interchange. The rain had stopped, but the sky was still gray and a fine mist scarved the dripping trees.

"Won't be long now," Nils remarked cheerfully.

They drove past a cluster of houses and a gas station, and then Nils turned suddenly onto a side road. It was a narrow strip of macadam that ran straight through a close-growing wilderness. Occasionally the forest opened to a tiny field where a shabby farmhouse squatted forlornly, but then, like a giant fist, the trees closed in again.

Incredibly bleak and alien-looking, it was hard to believe that land so desolate was only a four-hour drive from New York City. Lissa decided it was the ugliest countryside she'd ever seen. Pine Barrens was a good name for it!

Now and then a dark oily sheen of water glimmered through the thick undergrowth where a swamp bordered the road. She could imagine all sorts of slimey crawling things living in there. She felt a shiver of dread. This was even worse than she'd expected.

"Hah!" Nils' cry shattered her thoughts. "Here we are!"

He turned the truck suddenly onto a sandy track.

Tree branches scraped the sides like greedy clutching fingers as they bounced through deep ruts. Lissa clenched her fists in rising panic as they plunged deeper into the menacing green wilderness. *Oh, no!* she thought, *I don't want to live here....*

The track ended abruptly at a tiny clearing. There in front of them, crouched like a small frightened animal, stood the cabin. It looked like the photograph Nils and Barbara had showed her, and yet different. The photograph hadn't captured the great forest pressed all around with a dark brooding life of its own.

Nils switched off the ignition. The friendly rumble of the engine died away, leaving only a hushed and eerie silence.

"Well, now"—he breathed softly—"what do you think?"

Lissa looked at her father for a moment, hoping her despair didn't show too much. His merry laugh-crinkled eyes sparkled with enthusiasm.

I can't spoil it for them, she thought desperately. *It's their life, and they want it so much and everything, but ...*

"It looks—just like the picture." She tried to lie valiantly and fumbled with the door handle. "Come on, I want to see inside...."

Turning her face away from him, she flung herself out of the truck.

2

"Our new house!" Nils whooped.

With three great bounds he was out of the truck and standing by the door. Lissa felt an unpleasant squish of damp pine needles beneath her already-wet tennis shoes.

"Watch that first step," Nils warned. "It's a little rickety."

Barbara had just pulled in behind them in the VW and now joined them. Together they stepped through the door.

What Lissa saw was a big, low-ceilinged room with a stone fireplace yawning at one end. Several small windows gave only a greenish filtered light that seemed to struggle in through the surrounding forest. Barbara grabbed her hand.

"Come—I want to show you your room."

Lissa found herself being pulled to a small door beside the fireplace, and with dismay she looked into the little cubbyhole with rough wood walls and one tiny window.

"You'll be able to fix this up," Barbara told her, "It'll be really neat when you get your stuff arranged. Nils says he'll put in some shelves for you."

"Oh, Barbara . . ." Lissa's soft cry was anguished. Her mother hurried on.

"Here's the bathroom."

There was a stained, chipped sink, a john, and a big old-fashioned tub that stood on four clawed feet.

The kitchen was even worse. And the room where Nils and Barbara would sleep was hardly bigger than a closet.

"And here's where I'm going to have my workroom." Barbara pointed to a shedlike extension to the kitchen. "I'm going to put the kiln here," she waved her arm vaguely, "and my potter's wheel can go there. . . ."

It took less than five minutes to inspect the whole cabin.

"It doesn't look like much right now," Nils admitted, lounging in the doorway, "but just wait till we get it fixed up a bit. This was a gunning cabin—lots of hunters come here in the fall. . . ."

Lissa knew she wasn't hiding her feelings too well.

"Where's Dewey?" she asked.

"He wouldn't even get out of the car." Barbara laughed.

"I'll get him," Lissa said, and stumbled wordlessly out of the ugly little cabin.

From the back seat of the VW, Dewey gazed up at her with mournful brown eyes. A mongrel, part poodle and part sheep dog, he'd come from the city pound two years ago, undersized and worm-ridden. Now he was as fat as butter, and his curly black coat shone. Lissa threw her arms about him and laid her cheek against his fluffy chrysanthemum head.

"It's all right, boy," she whispered. "I'll take care of you."

Dewey steadfastly refused to leave his refuge on the back seat of the car. Finally, Lissa lifted him in her arms and set him down on the damp pine needles. He looked down in alarm and then up at Lissa in bewilderment. He was used to good solid cement under his feet.

Even Lissa had to laugh. She scooped him up once again, limp as a floppy stuffed animal, and carried him into the cabin. With a solid floor under him, Dewey seemed more relaxed. He began to explore the room cautiously, sniffing with his black button nose in corners where cobwebs clung, and sneezing now and then.

Meanwhile Nils had carried in the picnic basket and thermos and spread a checkered tablecloth on the dusty floor.

"We'll have lunch first," he announced, "and then unpack the truck."

Barbara spooned delicatessen potato salad onto paper plates and opened a plastic tub of fried chicken.

"Here's to our first meal in the woods!" Nils waved a drumstick in the air.

"Just think." Barbara sighed. "This time last week I was busy cataloguing a bunch of books, and you were selling golf clubs. . . ."

"Job slaves—fighting subway crowds and noise and rotten air," Nils added, and breathed deeply. "Ah, just smell it! This air!"

To Lissa it smelled of damp, wood rot, and dust. She nibbled at a chicken wing and tried not to think about anything.

Glancing at her parents, it seemed almost as if she were really seeing them for the first time. Two strangers. Strangers she'd known and loved and lived with all of her thirteen years.

Nils was a golden giant, humming and crackling with life. Everything he did was vigorous. And Barbara, with her long brown hair tied in a pony tail, a wash of pale freckles across her nose . . . gentle, vague, dreamy Barbara.

She'd never called them Mother and Dad. It was always Nils and Barbara. But who were they? Her parents, yes. But what were they all doing here, in this lost and lonely place?

Nils' voice broke into her confused thoughts.

"Okay—to work, you guys! I got to get that truck returned by the end of the day."

The rest of the afternoon passed in a blur. Grunting and straining, they unloaded the beds and the sofa, chairs and tables, and cartons of books, dishes, and clothes.

"By golly," Nils wheezed at one point, pausing to wipe his sweaty face, "we stayed too long in Brooklyn! We accumulated too much stuff!"

Barbara turned from the fireplace. She had just placed the old blue spatterware coffeepot on the

wooden mantleshelf. "Now I'm home," she said triumphantly.

Lissa knew the story of the coffeepot. In all of her parents' wanderings, Barbara always carried it, if nothing else. It had been a wedding gift from her mother in Pennsylvania, and wherever they went, the coffeepot made it home to her.

But this won't ever *be home for me,* Lissa thought grimly.

3

Lissa switched off her transistor radio and leaned back against the pillow, stretching her aching muscles. She wasn't used to such heavy work. Her body was exhausted, but her mind was throbbing.

Suddenly she became aware of the silence. It was a thick, heavy thing, a living presence. Even the insects that had buzzed and bumped against her window screen when the light was on had ceased their clamor.

Outside the dark was impenetrable. Threatening and mysterious, the great forest seemed to press in upon the frail cabin. She had pretended not to notice it as she helped unload the truck, for even in daylight the woods were dark. But at night they made a solid wall of blackness.

Lissa pulled the sheet up tighter and pressed her face into the pilow. Her thoughts turned to their bright apartment in Brooklyn, with the deep comfortable roar of the city always in the background, to familiar streets and the face of Marcy.

Marcy was the only real friend she'd ever had. In all the years of moving from place to place, Marcy was her first true friend.

Lissa was remembering the day she'd told Marcy they were leaving Brooklyn.

"You're kidding!" Marcy had exclaimed, her wise monkey face wrinkled in astonishment.

"I wish I were!" Lissa replied.

Marcy had hardly ever been out of Brooklyn, and she found Lissa's past travels glamorous.

"Maybe it won't be so bad—kinda like camp."

"What's so great about camp? Yecchh! It'll be awful, and you know it!"

"Well, maybe your parents won't like it, and they'll want to come back."

"Nils says it'll be a year at least," Lissa said gloomily. "He took a year's lease on this creepy cabin in the woods. He says we can't stand the rat race any longer —he's always going on about air pollution and noise and pressure and stuff. And it'll take at least a year to write the book he's planning to do."

"How about your mom? How does she feel about it?"

"Oh, you know Barbara. She always does anything Nils wants. She's going to make pots—remember that ceramics class she took last year? And she's really keen on going, too. . . . She loves camping and stuff like that."

"But—what about money? I mean, they'll have to give up their jobs and all."

Marcy's father worked in a bank, and she was a

regular tycoon about finance.

"They've saved enough, they say—for a year, anyway."

"Well, at least you won't starve." And then Marcy's face brightened a bit. "And you know, Lissa, it might be good for your writing—kinda like Thoreau at Walden."

She always insisted that Lissa become a writer, on the strength of her book reports at school. Because Lissa always had her nose in a book and wrote the best reports in the seventh grade, Marcy figured that her friend's future lay in literature. As for herself, Marcy had decided to become the head of a giant cosmetics company. "I'm not pretty enough to be a model," she'd said, "but boy, just look at the fortune Helena Rubinstein's made! I'm going to have a big office on Fifth Avenue and a penthouse on Central Park, an' you can come and live with me."

A heavy weight landed on Lissa's stomach, wrenching her thoughts back to the present. Dewey, who had not budged from the cabin all day, grunted and began trampling her in his three-times circle before he settled to sleep. Lissa reached out and gathered him close, finding a familiar comfort in his warm shaggy bulk.

Now her thoughts ranged farther back.

She didn't really remember Denver, where she'd been born, and she remembered only dim fragments of Norway, where she'd lived till she was four. Nils had taken them back to his homeland, which he'd left when he was sixteen. His parents lived on a small mountain farm, and Lissa could remember snatches of glistening white winters, her grandparents' ruddy faces, the small friendly herd of goats, and the smell of coffee always simmering on a huge black stove.

Then it was back to America, and a small town in Vermont where Nils worked as a ski instructor for a couple of years. She started school there, and there was skiing, and swimming in a cold lake, and brief, bright, berry-picking summers.

Finally, they moved to New York, and how many apartments? Lissa tried to tick them off in her mind— Greenwich Village, smelly and noisy, and then two in the Bronx, and finally Brooklyn. Brooklyn and Marcy for two whole wonderful years!

Barbara worked in the Public Library, and Nils held an honest-to-goodness job in a sporting goods store. They lived like real people for a while.

And now . . . there was this, this miserable cabin huddled in the vast, dreary, lonely South Jersey Pine Barrens!

Lissa pulled the sheet over her head and stifled a sob.

4

"You can't miss it," Nils said the next morning, handing Lissa the rough map he'd drawn. "Just go down the road about a mile, turn right—it's the first road you come to—and then two more miles into town."

Lissa put the map into her bike basket. They needed bread and milk, and she'd been delegated to the errand. The nearest town was called Green Bank, three miles away.

She had to walk her bike down the long lane, for the ruts were deep and still soggy from yesterday's rain. But at least today the sun was shining. It filtered through the tall pines and lay in scattered fragments on the glistening forest floor.

Biking was easy once she reached the macadam road. The road was flat and smooth, and not a single car passed as she pedaled along. The only sound was the silky whoosh of her bike tires, and an occasional birdcall, sharp and clear. And, she had to admit, the air smelled delicious, a sweet resiny scent of wet pine drying in the sun.

But the woods still seemed menacing. They closed in the road, making it almost like a tunnel. Lissa had read a story about the Jersey Devil, and even though she knew it was fiction, she couldn't help an apprehensive glance now and then into the depths of the surrounding trees.

According to the legend, long ago, not far from here, there lived a farm woman called Mother Leeds. Like the old woman in the shoe, she had too many children. When she found that once again she was pregnant, she cried out a curse and offered the unborn baby to the devil. When it was born, on a stormy night in winter, the child had horns, cloven feet, and a forked tail. And as it grew, it began to ravage the surrounding countryside, terrifying the good folk, stealing sheep and even babies. It left a trail of blood and terror down through two centuries, and even now, every once in a while, strange stories were told of torn or missing farm animals and of huge footprints left in the earth.

With such thoughts on her mind, Lissa nearly missed the turn. She braked sharply, skidded to a stop, and checked her map. Because of this she was past the strange old house before she fully became aware of it. Braking again, she turned her bike in a circle and went back to make sure of that fleeting edge-of-the-eye vision.

There it was, all by itself, just at the corner where the two roads met.

The house was black. It was not painted black, but weathered so, layered with ancient cedarwood shingles.

The gables, roof, and sides seemed to be all of a piece, one flowing into the other. Cracked dark green blinds gave it a secret, shuttered look, with a foam of lace curtain showing at the bottom. It looked like an Andrew Wyeth painting.

But the creepy thing was not the house.

Beside it, in the yard, a huge old iron pot hung steaming on a tripod, and over it bent the figure of an old woman. Wisps of gray hair stood up from her head, moving in the heat from the crackling fire. She was stirring the pot with a long-handled wooden paddle, her back to the road.

Lissa stared for one long startled moment.

The old woman straightened, turned, and stared directly at Lissa, a frown wrinkling her pasty face.

Lissa's heart gave a great leap.

Hastily she turned and biked away as fast as she could, pedals flying. When she'd sped along for about a mile, she finally slowed down a bit, her breath still unsteady.

That's ridiculous, she told herself sternly. *It couldn't have been Mother Leeds. She's been dead for over two hundred years. And it's only a legend, anyway.*

But who was the old woman? She certainly looked like a real witch, with the iron pot and all.

Up ahead Lissa suddenly saw a cluster of houses lining the road, each surrounded by huge old trees. The road curved sharply just then, and Lissa caught her breath. There in front of her lay a shining river, sunlight dancing on its rippling surface. She saw a

funny old wooden bridge, and beside it a weathered building with a faded sign that read SIMPKINS STORE.

So this was Green Bank.

5

The old store was cool and quiet as Lissa stepped through a patched screen door. Ancient floorboards creaked beneath her feet, and a curious scent mixed of apples and kerosene filled the air.

By the freezer chest a dumpy girl in faded red pants was pawing among ice-cream bars. She looked up, her eyes meeting Lissa's for a second. She glanced quickly away.

Lissa found a rack of packaged bread and a case by the wall where milk was stored. She carried her groceries to the counter and set them down. The small weathered-looking woman at the cash register was talking to a boy leaning against the counter.

"Hear it's been a busy summer over to Batsto, Jess," she was saying.

"Yeah, Aunt Sally. Lots of tourists, especially on weekends."

She chortled.

"How ya like drivin' the stagecoach?"

"Sure beats cleaning the stable, like I did last year."
He laughed.

He straightened suddenly and looked down at Lissa.

It was a delightful surprise—a boy who could look *down* at her! Lissa was always self-conscious about her height. Already five feet six, it seemed to her that she was never going to stop growing. She hated towering over everyone her own age, especially boys.

"Hi!" the boy said, smiling.

Lissa returned his smile with surprise.

"Hi," she replied, and then, because he seemed friendly and because curiosity overcame her shyness, she asked, "Do you really drive a *stagecoach?*"

He chuckled and held up his hand.

"Honest truth!"

"But—"

"I work over at Batsto in the summer," he explained, obviously enjoying her puzzled expression. "It's a restored village, about five miles from here. You know, sort of like Williamsburg, only not so big and elegant. It was an iron and glassmaking town once—they made cannonballs for the Revolution there, from local bog iron."

"Oh, I see. And the stagecoach?"

"I make runs with it through the village, mostly for little kids to ride. They love it."

"Sounds like fun."

"It is," he said.

Suddenly he thrust out his hand and shook hers in a firm grip. It was an old-fashioned gesture and caught her by surprise.

"Jess Cowperthwaite." He pronounced his name slurringly. It sounded like "Coppathwet."

Lissa like his warm, strong grip.

"I'm Lissa Evorssen," she said.

"Pleased to meet you. You a summer visitor?"

"No. I'm going to live here for a little while."

She told him about the cabin.

"Oh, yeah." He nodded. "I know the place."

"We'll be going back to New York next year," Lissa said.

She'd decided that if she said it often enough it would come true.

The dumpy girl came over and joined them.

"Hey, Helen-Ann," Jess said. "Meet Lissa. She's going to be living near here."

The girl nodded shyly, returning Lissa's greeting. Overweight, with stringy brown hair and a lopsided smile, she seemed awkward and ill at ease.

Lissa paid for her purchases and started for the door, unable to think of anything more to say. Then she had a sudden thought and turned back.

"Jess," she said. "Back down the road, at the corner, there's a big black house, set 'way back. I saw an old woman—"

Jess grinned. "Oh, that was Mrs. G."

"Gee?"

"Her name's Mrs. Gilfillan, but everyone mostly calls her Mrs. G."

"She was cooking something in a big pot," Lisa said, "and I thought—oh, this sounds crazy, but—she looked like a—a witch—"

Behind the counter Aunt Sally gave a small snort. Jess frowned.

Oh-oh, Lissa thought, *I must've said something wrong.*

"Witch?" Jess looked stern. "Well, hardly—"

Aunt Sally laughed outright, and a strange expression crossed Helen-Ann's face.

"Jess always gets mad when anyone mean-mouths Mrs. G.," Helen-Ann said to Lissa.

"I do not," he snapped. "And anyway, Lissa doesn't know."

But he still looked annoyed as he walked to the door and held it open for Lissa.

"Mrs. G. is just about the most interesting person around here," he said, turning his back to Helen-Ann and Aunt Sally. "She's . . . different, that's all. And kind of hard to get to know at first. But she's really a great person—take my word for it."

"I'm sorry." Lissa felt awkward again. "I didn't mean—"

"If she had her kettle out she was probably dying wool. She makes rugs to sell, and she mixes her own dyes and things."

Jess headed down the road by the river.

"One day maybe I'll take you over to meet her," he called over his shoulder. "So long now—see you around!"

Behind her in the store Lissa could hear whispering and soft laughter from Helen-Ann and Aunt Sally.

6

On the way home, Lissa's thoughts were racing as fast as her bike pedals. She put Helen-Ann and Aunt Sally out of her mind, and the old witch woman was so eerie and strange that Lissa decided, in spite of Jess' offer, that she didn't ever want to meet her. It was much more fun to think about Jess.

She'd always had trouble talking to boys, but Jess was different. She tried to picture him again. He was all a comfortable brown, like autumn leaves—tan chinos and shirt blending with his tanned skin, russet hair, and sherry-colored eyes. And tall! Oh, bliss!

At school the boys started calling her The Flagpole, because she towered over everyone. In fact, that was the beginning of her friendship with Marcy, when she came charging to Lissa's defense on the playground. She could hardly wait to tell Marcy about Jess.

Lissa always said she didn't like boys.

"They think they're so darn superior," she said many times.

But deep inside, someplace secret and dark, she dreamed.

There was a boy in her class last year, tall and scornful, a loner too. She used to watch him covertly and wrote his name on her notebook paper, then tore it to tiny bits and flushed it down the john.

And now, here she was, all alone again, having to start all over again. Jess had seemed friendly. Helen-Ann looked a little weird, but maybe she'd turn out to be okay.

I wonder when I'll see them again, Lissa thought. *Maybe I'll go back to the store tomorrow—I'll offer to do all the shopping from now on. . . .*

Hisss——sss!

The sound was like an angry snake's.

Lissa leaped.

The bike wobbled crazily, and she landed in a tangled heap on the road, the upended front wheel still spinning.

Quickly and fearfully she looked around for the snake, but the road lay still and empty. Then she saw a big ugly piece of glass sticking in the front tire. It was a blowout.

Lissa painfully crawled out from under the fallen bike and hauled herself to her feet. There was a big rip in her jeans and a lot of blood from nasty brush burns on her knee and elbow.

"Oh, damn and blast," she muttered, as she began gathering up the scattered loaves of bread and milk cartons.

Just then she was startled by a voice.

"You'd better come in and wash those cuts."

Lissa whirled around and found herself facing her worst fear. The witchlike old woman was standing there, half hidden by a bush. Behind her the tall black house loomed like a bad dream.

Lissa fought back panic and swallowed hard.

"I—I'll be all right."

"Nonsense. You're bleeding. Come."

It was an order, barked in a crisp voice.

Lissa pulled her bike to the side of the road and slowly followed the old woman up the path toward the forbidding house.

Her heart was beating like a trapped bird's, and she'd never felt so scared in her whole life. It was like a nightmare, where you have to go on doing things you don't want to do, powerless to help yourself.

She glanced fearfully at the figure ahead of her. The old woman was tall, thin almost to the point of emaciation, her rain-colored hair caught in a wispy knot, and wearing a dress of the 1930's style in faded flowered cotton.

This can't be happening to me, she thought numbly.

They crossed a creaking splintery porch hung heavy with vines, and then Lissa found herself entering a kitchen. But such a kitchen!

Racks at each window rioted with flowering plants— it was like a greenhouse. Bunches of dried herbs hung from the ceiling, sending off a subtle fragrance. Against one wall stood an antique pump organ, and shelves of books and china filled the others.

"Come over to the sink and wash those cuts," the old

woman commanded.

Cool water felt good on the stinging wounds, patted dry with a soft linen towel.

Mrs. G. made no further attempt at conversation as she applied an aromatic salve to the brush burns.

"There . . . now," she said, wiping her fingers.

For the first time, Lissa found herself looking directly into two piercing gray eyes behind rimless glasses.

"Th—thank you," she mumbled. "That feels g— good."

"Do you have far to go?"

"N—no, ma'am. Just down the road."

"Well, then, be off with you. And next time be more careful."

It was a clear dismissal. Lissa fled without another word, not even looking back.

She got her bike, picked out the piece of glass from the flattened tire, and hurried as fast as she could down the lonely road toward the cabin.

7

For the next few days Lissa was too busy to think much about the strange old woman, for she was occupied with fixing up her room. Nils remarked, with a certain disapproval, that Lissa had a strong nesting instinct.

"Everywhere we go, you burrow in and make yourself a cubbyhole," he told her, then laughed and rumpled her hair. "What are you afraid of, *min elskling?* The world is wide and wonderful—don't always try to hide yourself from it!"

Well, maybe that was true. Nils had a great natural curiosity, and he made friends easily, Lissa thought half in admiration and half in exasperation. But it's different with me. I need someplace that is just mine. Her room, wherever they went, was always her refuge.

So the cabin in the silent forest rang with the sound of saw and hammer as Nils cheerfully built shelves to Lissa's specifications. A plain pine plank made a good desk, and her bed occupied the other wall of the little room.

Her portable sewing machine whirred busily as she stitched yellow gingham curtains for the window. She arranged her books on the shelves, along with the collection of whimsical pottery animals Barbara had made for her. Big posters tacked to the bare walls looked cheerful, and Curious George, the funny plush monkey Marcy had given her last Christmas, perched on the headboard of her bed.

Now, standing in the doorway, surveying her very own room, Lissa heaved a small sigh of content. Dewey lay curled in the middle of the bed, and Lissa sat down beside him, gathering his woolly warmth in her arms.

"Hey, it's not too bad, is it, old boy!"

Dewey licked her hand and laid his furry head on her arm. She burrowed her face against his.

"Maybe now we can hack it," she whispered. "It's only for a year anyway, and then we'll be going back to Brooklyn."

Lissa had told her parents about her adventure at the store and with Mrs. G., but they were busy with their own projects and didn't seem too interested. Barbara was absorbed in setting up her potter's shed, and now her wheel was humming most of the day. Nils had met a man who took him fishing on the river every day, and his typewriter stood silent on the living room table.

The weather continued in the fine crystal clearness of June.

Nils had repaired her bike tire, and twice Lissa had made the trip to Green Bank to the store, but neither time did she see Jess or Helen-Ann.

Though Nils urged her to explore the woods, she was still afraid. She'd read about the poisonous snakes of South Jersey and about packs of wild dogs reported to roam the depths of the woods. And the little sandy trails that crisscrossed the forest all looked the same to her, leading nowhere but into more dark trees.

But by Saturday morning Lissa was getting desperate. Her room was finished, the cabin was in order, she'd already written three letters to Marcy, and there was simply nothing to do. Finally, she decided to bake brownies. It was her one cooking accomplishment.

As she was mixing the flour and sugar and chocolate together, an idea struck.

Her heart gave a funny little leap at first. *But then— why not,* she thought.

She didn't bite me.

In fact, she was kind.

And, it's a way of saying thank you.

When the brownies were baked, Lissa cut them into squares and arranged them carefully on a paper plate, covering it with Saran wrap. She tied a bit of lilac ribbon around it and wrote a note on her prettiest notepaper:

> Thank you for helping me the other day. I appreciate your kindness.
>
> Sincerely yours,
> LISSA EVORSSEN

She'd just leave it on Mrs. G.'s doorstep. She'd go up quietly, leave the gift, and slip away without being seen.

At the end of the lane, Lissa noticed a clump of daisies growing by the road. She stopped, gathered a few, and tucked them into the lilac-ribbon bow.

The road was empty, and pedaling along in the warm June sunlight, Lissa felt a strange happiness. Over her head a hawk sailed and dipped, and a little wind sighed softly through the trees. Daisies and some tiny yellow flowers she didn't recognize starred the road's edge, catching sun like a scattering of golden dollars, and the air smelled fresh and piny and sweet.

When she arrived at the tall black house, Lissa left her bike at the road and looked about carefully. The place seemed deserted—blank and faceless. She felt wary, however, as she approached the vine-hung porch.

She set the plate on the top step. Still there was no sound or movement from within.

Lissa turned quickly to leave, when all of a sudden a gray shadow darted from under the step.

Startled, she jumped back with a low cry. "Oh."

A large silver-colored tail disappeared into the shrubbery.

Lisa began to run down the path.

"Stop!"

She froze.

"What are you doing here?"

The voice behind her was cold and harsh.

8

By the time Lissa had turned slowly around, her heart pounding, Mrs. G. stood on the porch step holding the gift. She was looking at it curiously.

"What's this?"

"It's—I—uh—baked brownies," Lissa faltered. "There's—a note . . ."

She just stood there unable to move as the old woman adjusted her glasses and read the note.

There seemed to be a softening of expression on her stern face, but Lissa was too nervous to be sure. There was a long silence.

"Well, then, come in."

"Oh, no! I mean, I didn't . . ."

"Don't just stand there, child. Come in."

Once again, much against her better judgment, Lissa found herself in the big kitchen.

"Sit down." Mrs. G. pointed to a tall stool.

Lissa sat.

The old woman went to the stove, where a kettle was

already boiling. She began to spoon tea leaves into a brown pot.

"We'll have a cup of tea and taste these brownies," she announced. "Will you please get some cups from the shelf there."

From a bewildering array of antique china, Lissa selected two cups of paper-thin porcelain, milky-white with tiny bluish dots.

"Ah, you like the rice china!" Mrs. G. observed. "So do I."

She laid a bony finger on one of the minute transparent-looking dots on the saucer.

"See? The Chinese potters place rice grains in the clay before firing it."

"They're lovely," Lissa said. "They must be very old."

"These cups are, but the china is still being made. Now—will you clear off that end of the table."

Lissa removed a pile of books and newspapers, recognizing with surprise the *New York Times Book Review*. This was certainly an amazing place!

Mrs. G. poured the tea, strange-looking, straw-colored, and with a faintly smoky odor.

"Green tea," she explained briefly.

Lissa took a tentative sip. It tasted pungent and slightly bitter. Mrs. G. was watching her with a curious expression.

"It's—uh—interesting."

The old woman laughed sharply. It was a rusty sound, as if she didn't laugh often.

"Ha! It's got a taste that must be cultivated. But

cautiously. There are some who claim it can cause hallucinations if drunk in quantity. There's a story by Sheridan Le Fanu called 'Green Tea.'" She paused, looking intently at Lissa.

"Do you like to read?"

"I—oh, yes! *Love* to!"

"Good. I'm glad to hear that. I have many books." She gestured to the overflowing shelves, with other books piled on chairs and on the floor. "There's no public library near here, so you may borrow some of these if you like."

Lissa, feeling bewildered, didn't quite know what to say. Mrs. G.'s voice was surprising too, not raspy, but dry, clear, and precise.

"Now, Lissa Evorssen, did you just spring like a wood nymph from a tree, or are you a person with a family?"

Lissa took another gulp of tea.

"I'm a person with a family," she replied, and discovered that she was smiling. Anyone with that many books couldn't be too bad.

"We just moved here . . ."

She found herself suddenly talking, telling Mrs. G. about Nils and Barbara and the cabin.

"We'll just be staying for a year," she repeated the magic formula. "And then we're going back to New York. My best friend, Marcy, lives there."

The old woman listened attentively, sipping her tea and making no comment.

"You don't know anyone here?" she queried when Lissa finished.

"No. Well, that is, I did meet a boy at the store—Jess Cowperthwaite."

For the first time a shadow of a smile crossed Mrs. G.'s stern face.

"Ah—Jess."

"He seems . . . very nice." Lissa felt a faint flush of color in her cheeks.

Mrs. G. nodded.

"He is that. There have been Cowperthwaites in Green Bank for three hundred years. Jess' father is a ranger in the Wharton State Forest here, and that is what Jess is planning to be. You can learn a lot about the woods from that boy."

Lissa was quite sure that she didn't want to learn anything about these woods, but she nodded anyway.

"Did you ever see a cranberry bog?" Mrs. G. asked suddenly.

Surprised by the abrupt change of subject, Lissa merely shook her head. She would much rather have gone on talking about Jess.

The old woman stood up.

"Well, there's no time like the present. Come along."

Lissa followed her out of the house and down an overgrown path behind it running along the edge of the woods.

"My husband operated these cranberry bogs years ago," Mrs. G. explained as they walked along. "Now they're abandoned and gone wild again."

"I thought cranberries came in cans," Lissa said with a laugh, and then quickly added, "Oh, I'm joking, of course."

Mrs. G. pointed out certain trees and wild flowers as they went along. She touched a bush with small glossy dark-green leaves.

"This is *Gaylussacia dumosa*—wild huckleberry. Next month you can gather the berries. They're delicious, like blueberries, only sweeter and more woodsy-flavored. And here, see this little low plant?—that's teaberry. Break a leaf and bite it."

Lissa did as she was told.

"Why," she cried, "it tastes like teaberry chewing gum!"

"This leaf is where the flavor comes from," Mrs. G. told her.

Lissa learned that the tall coarse ferns that grew beside the path were called bracken, *Pteridium aquilinum latiusculum.*

"I like the old Latin names," Mrs. G. said. "They have a good rolling sound on the tongue. And it keeps my mind working—learning them. Ah—here we are now."

Through a break in the trees, Lissa could see a great open field with an earthen wall at one end, and beyond it another field.

"Just go over to the edge and bend down—careful, it's marshy."

Lissa did as directed and close up could see that the whole field was covered with a tight low-growing mat of tiny leaved plants, almost like fine ferns.

"Oh, I see the little berries now, she called. "But they're green."

"They'll be ripe and red in the fall," Mrs. G. explained. "We always used to harvest in October, by flooding the bogs—see the dam down there?—and floating the berries, then gathering them in wooden scoops."

There was a faraway look in her gray eyes behind their rimless glasses.

"Those were busy days here, then, when my husband was alive. Trucks coming and going all day, and the Pines people coming in from miles around to help gather the harvest for market."

Later in the afternoon, when she left for home, Lissa had a worn copy of *David Copperfield* under her arm and a bunch of wild roses for Barbara.

"I really had a good time," she said to Mrs. G., and then, surprised at her own boldness, added, "May I come again sometime?"

A shuttered look closed over the old woman's face.

"Well," she said harshly. "We shall see."

9

"She's really neat!" Lissa said enthusiastically. "Jess was right. She's a little scary—I never met anyone at all like her before—but she's just about the most interesting person. . . ."

They were sitting at the supper table, and Lissa was telling her parents about Mrs. G.

"If Oliver—that's her cat—hadn't jumped out at me, I might never even have met her." Lissa laughed. "Boy, was I ever scared!"

She helped herself to more salad.

"She told me that Oliver was a stray kitten—she calls him Oliver after Oliver Twist—she's a real Dickens fan. He'd been so badly mistreated that it took her weeks even to get him to come into the house. He won't come near anyone but her. Someday I hope I'll actually get to see all of him—I just caught a glimpse of his tail today."

Nils went to the stove for another plate of spaghetti.

"Funny you should meet her," he said over his

shoulder. "This guy I was fishing with was talking about her today. I told him about her fixing your arm. Folks around here pretty much leave her alone. He said she's kind of strange."

"How do you mean strange?" Barbara asked.

"Well, for one thing, she's not a native here. And for the Pineys that means strange," Nils chuckled. "Fella said she and her husband came here from Philadelphia about forty years ago and bought up some cranberry bogs. Set themselves up as gentry, I guess, and that didn't go down too well with the natives."

"What happened?" Lissa was eager to hear more. Nils shrugged.

"Nothing much. He died, and she just stayed on and let the bogs go. They lost their money, and she just scrapes along somehow."

"Does she have any children?" Barbara queried.

"A daughter, but I gather she went off a long time ago—lives in California, I think the man said."

"That's kind of sad," Lissa remarked thoughtfully.

"This guy said the old lady never leaves her place, except once a year, to go to the Crafts Festival at Batsto. She makes hooked rugs and sells them there."

Nils waved his fork at Barbara.

"Hey! That gives me an idea! Why don't we take some of your pottery over to the festival? It's next week. A really big deal around here, they tell me. A lot of rich tourists come in—they tour the village, and there are booths where you can sell stuff."

"I don't have very much made yet," Barbara said, but her eyes were sparkling.

"Well, you've got a whole week. And we'll help, won't we, Lissa?"

"Sure, it might be fun!" Lissa caught some of their enthusiasm.

"But what about your book, Nils?" Barbara asked. "After all, that's the main reason we came here."

"Oh, I've got plenty of time for that—have to absorb some local color, you know." He laughed, pushing back his chair excitedly. "Tell you what. I'll just take a run over to Batsto right now and see about getting us a booth. Now you two get cracking. . . ."

Later that night Lissa closed *David Copperfield* at page 64. It was really a *good* book. She switched off her light. Somehow tonight the dark didn't seem quite so dark. The silence was kind of peaceful, like a quiet-flowing stream.

She snuggled into her pillow, Dewey a warm weight on her feet. She was thinking about Mrs. G. and Oliver, over across the dark forest. She wondered what they were doing in the tall black house.

And then she thought about the coming festival at Batsto. Maybe, with luck, she might even see Jess there. When she wrote to Marcy tomorrow, she'd have a lot to tell her.

Lissa was smiling as she drifted off to sleep.

10

"Lissa! Come here!"

Lissa sat bolt upright, jolted from sleep.

"Hurry!"

Without even stopping to pull on her bathrobe, Lissa ran into the living room, rubbing her eyes.

Barbara stood by the window. She grabbed Lissa's arm, pulling her closer, and pointed.

"Look."

Through the glass Lissa could see the small clearing in front of the cabin, colorless in the early-dawn light. A large animal was thrashing around out there, running in half-circles, falling, and staggering up again with awful moaning sounds.

"It's Dewey," Barbara cried. "I don't know what's wrong."

In the dim light Lissa strained to see. Flecks of foam feathered the dog's mouth. He began to crawl on his belly toward the cabin steps, whimpering.

Lissa stared in horror at her mother.

"What happened?"

"I don't know—I just let him out a few minutes ago, and he was all right then."

"Where's Nils?"

"He's gone—went out early, before daylight—he said something about going fishing."

Barbara's eyes were puzzled.

"I wonder if Dewey could be . . . rabid? If he might have been bitten by a squirrel or something?"

Lissa looked out the window again at the dog who now lay still, his head on the cabin step.

"I—I don't know," she replied shakily. "He's not very smart about the woods."

"Well, we've got to do something," Barbara said. "Oh, how I wish we had a phone! If he *is* rabid, even if we had a gun—which we don't—I couldn't bring myself to use it."

Lissa's heart contracted sharply.

"I'm going out to see—"

Barbara gripped her arm firmly.

"The heck you are! It could be dangerous."

"Dewey won't bite me," Lissa said.

But she wasn't really sure. She didn't know anything about rabid dogs.

"We'll both go," Barbara said quietly. "But we'd better put on jackets and gloves—that'll be some protection if he does try to bite."

In a couple of minutes, with jackets over their pajamas, and booted and gloved, they opened the cabin door cautiously.

Then the odor hit them full in the face. It was like a

physical blow.

Pure, overpowering, undiluted . . . skunk!

They'd never smelled anything so strong.

Gagging, and covering their noses with their hands, they approached Dewey. He looked up at them through glazed eyes and thumped his tail feebly once.

"Poor boy," Lissa murmured. "Don't worry—we'll help you."

She looked down at Barbara, who was kneeling and stroking his head.

"You'd better go for help," Barbara said. "I don't s'pose there's a vet near here, but try to find a phone and look in the Yellow Pages."

"I'll try Mrs. G.'s—she's the nearest."

"Okay," Barbara replied. "I'll get a blanket to cover him and a bowl of water for him. He must have met a skunk and got sprayed right in the face. . . . Phew! Its incredible!"

Lissa was already in her room, pulling on jeans and a shirt.

"I hope he won't die. I think he's too weak to move."

"I'll stay with him till you get back, and Lissa— hurry!"

"At first there was no answer to Lissa's knock on Mrs. G.'s back door, and she had almost despaired when it finally did open. The old woman wore a faded woolen bathrobe and her rain-colored hair was tousled. She looked very cross.

"What on earth—"

"Oh, Mrs. G.—I'm sorry if I wakened you—but I need help!"

"Well, come in. Don't just stand there hopping about."

When Lissa told her what had happened, Mrs. G. looked thoughtful for a moment.

"Will he die?" Lissa asked.

"I hardly think so," the old woman said dryly. "Do you have any canned tomatoes?"

Lissa gaped at her.

"Canned tomatoes?" She wondered if the old woman had suddenly lost her senses. "What's that got to do with Dewey?"

Mrs. G. smiled at Lissa's expression.

"I don't know why—probably something to do with the balance between acidity and alkalinity. We don't have time to go into that just now. But they do work. Wait here."

Lissa stood in bewilderment as Mrs. G. vanished down the cellar steps. She reappeared in a few minutes with an armful of mason jars filled with canned tomatoes.

"Now," she said, "just pour these over the dog and rub them in good."

"You're putting me on!"

A frown appeared on the old woman's face, and her eyes snapped.

"Do as you're told," she said sharply. "And hurry! That dog's in misery."

The bike ride back to the cabin was the longest of Lissa's life. *Tomatoes!* she thought crossly. *That's really crazy! What good will that do? I should have hunted up a phone and called a vet. Maybe the people around here are right. Mrs. G. really is strange!*

Dewey lay under the blanket with his head in Barbara's lap. And the smell was still awful!

"Did you find a vet?"

"No, and you'll never believe this," Lissa answered, helping her mother to remove the blanket, "but . . ."

She emptied a jar of tomatoes on Dewey's back. She expected him to snarl at her, but he just lay there looking up helplessly.

Barbara stared at her in disbelief.

"She say's it'll work," Lissa said, "but personally I think she's really flipped out."

They continued pouring until all the jars were empty, working the gooey red pulp into his fur with their fingers. At last Dewey heaved a gigantic sigh and pulled himself slowly to his feet. He tried without success to shake.

It was amazing!

The skunky smell had diminished. They could all breathe again without gagging.

Lissa hunkered back on her heels and looked at the dripping dog. Then suddenly, in relief, she began to laugh.

"He looks like a . . . a furry pizza!"

Barbara began to laugh too.

"Oh, dear," she cried finally, wiping her eyes, "this just can't be for real!"

Dewey was trying to lick the sticky tomato mess, and he was a picture of bewilderment. Lissa doubled up again in laughter. She caught him up and hugged him to her.

"Oh, you funny old city dog!" she gasped.

Later, Barbara ran a tub of warm water, liberally loaded with jasmine bath salts. Dewey drooped in humiliation and defeat and allowed himself to be scrubbed and toweled. Subdued, and smelling like a flower garden, he was peacefully asleep in a patch of sun when Nils arrived home at suppertime.

Lissa wrote to Marcy that night:

I had to carry my clothes on the end of a stick—it was my gorgeous new bandanna shirt, too!—and bury them out in the woods. You can't believe how scared I was at first! But now you'll know, if you ever meet up with a skunk in the park—ha! canned tomatoes really do work! This is sure a crazy place to live!

And she ended the letter as always:

I miss you so much. I feel so darn lonely—oh, I do wish you were here!!!

JULY

The day of the Crafts Festival dawned brilliant with sun. Lissa and Barbara were up early to wrap the pottery in newspaper and pack it in cardboard cartons.

The festival committee had asked Nils if Barbara would also like to bring her potter's wheel and give demonstrations during the day. So Nils tied the bulky wheel to the roof of the VW and made the first trip to Batsto by himself.

Lissa had made matching long skirts for herself and Barbara from an old India-print bedspread. She spent an extra-long time brushing her hair that morning and used the pale lipstick she kept for special occasions.

"How do I look?" she asked Nils when he returned.

"Beautiful, *min elskling!*" he cried, catching her up and swinging her around.

They decided to leave Dewey outside for the day, sure he wouldn't stray far from the cabin. Since his encounter with the skunk, he hadn't ventured away from the clearing. Lissa put a bowl of water and a handful of dog biscuits on the step, hugged him, and turned her back resolutely on his woeful look as they drove away.

The parking lot at Batsto was already beginning to fill with cars as they pulled in. Nils guided them to one of the restored workers' cottages that stood along the main road of the village. Behind a picket fence in its small yard the potter's wheel was already set up. Lissa began to arrange Barbara's finished pieces on a rough wooden table, while Barbara prepared wet clay for the demonstration.

"Why don't you go and look around before it gets crowded," Nils suggested. "I'll finish this."

"Okay. I won't be long."

Lissa had gone only a short distance when she saw a familiar figure. Mrs. G. was sitting in a folding canvas chair in one of the cottage yards. Bright many-colored hooked rugs hung on the fence.

Lissa waved and walked up to her.

"Hello," she said shyly. "Your rugs are beautiful."

"Why, Lissa! Whatever are you doing here?"

"Barbara brought her pottery."

"Hi, there, you two! Getting ready for a big day?"

Lissa spun around.

Jess was standing there, grinning at them. He looked kind of odd in baggy homespun trousers, a white collarless shirt, and a broadbrimmed black hat.

Mrs. G. studied him with approval.

"You look just fine," she said, smiling at him. "You know, you've got a good, strong old-fashioned nose."

Jess laughed.

"That's just a nice way of saying I've got the big Cowperthwaite nose."

"No shame in that," she retorted.

Lissa could sense the genuine affection between them. She felt suddenly left out.

"I think I'll take a look around before the crowd starts," she said.

She walked away abruptly, her earlier happiness diminished. Once she glanced back over her shoulder, half hoping Jess would be following her, but he still stood talking with Mrs. G.

So who needs you? she thought, and held her head very high.

But soon, in spite of her wounded feelings, Lissa became fascinated by the sights around her.

The village of Batsto lay nestled in the curve of a small river in the heart of the Pine Barrens. Brown cedar water sheeted down the huge creaking wheel of the sawmill on its banks. Farther up the road stood the ironmaster's great mansion, like a fantastic vine-shrouded castle with its gables and turrets scrolled with carved wood.

She inspected the great shadowy stone barns smelling fragrant with new hay and stopped by a pen where ornamental ducks, geese, and peacocks strutted, pecking at corn. The village store was a treasurehouse—bolts of calico, horse harness, barrels of crackers, tobacco and seeds. Lissa bought a handful of barley-sugar sticks.

The crowds were growing now, and there was a happy holiday bustle in the air as Lissa made her way back along the road. She heard a tremendous rattle and a jingle of harness and quickly stepped out of the way.

"Ho-ahh!"

Jess was on the driver's seat of an old red stagecoach, expertly flicking the reins to guide the horses. From inside she could hear delighted whoops from the children. He didn't see her, and the coach rumbled on down the road.

Already a small crowd of people was gathered around Barbara at her potter's wheel, which whirred as she deftly shaped a pot.

Nils shook a small box as Lissa joined him.

"Hey! We made some sales already," he cried. "You take over here for a while. I want to look around."

The morning passed quickly for Lissa as the festival crowds increased. It was pleasant sitting under a dappled old sycamore tree in the early-July sunlight. The visitors were leisurely and friendly, in a holiday mood, and as she wrapped the pottery they bought and made change from the box, she found herself talking with them easily, like a Pine Barrens native.

"Oh, yes," she said to a man, "they made cannon-balls for the Revolution right here, from the bog iron. . . ."

"No, ma'am, you can't get cranberries 'til fall—they're harvested in October. . . ."

"Just follow this road—the sawmill's right down there. . . ."

At noon, when Nils returned, Lissa was glowing.

"Look—we have only four pieces left!"

"What a salesperson!" he said with a laugh, and added, "Say, I have a message for you. I stopped to talk to your Mrs. G., and she's invited you to share a sandwich with her."

"Really?" Lissa was stunned.

"Go ahead. You've done enough work for one day. . . ."

Before he finished, Lissa was running down the road.

12

Lissa and Mrs. G. shared a loaf of homemade bread spread thick with spicy apple butter, chunks of sharp cheese, and a thermos of tea. As they ate, Mrs. G. told Lissa the history of the old town.

"It's hard to believe, but about eight hundred people lived here once," she said. "There are a lot of these lost towns, ghost towns really, scattered through the Pines. They flourished for a few years and then disappeared— only a few overgrown cellar holes left. Batsto was luckier—saved before it was completely gone. The woods have a way of swallowing things. You know, this is the last authentic bit of wilderness left on the entire seaboard."

Lissa shivered in the warm sunlight, then said, "The Pine Barrens are such a mysterious kind of place."

Mrs. G. nodded in agreement.

"Most people don't even know they exist. It's like a whole lost world here, haunting and beautiful. . . . It can capture your heart."

Then a hint of a smile crinkled Mrs. G.'s eyes.

"Why don't you take a ride on the stagecoach?"

Lissa flushed.

"Oh, I'm too old for that."

"Nonsense! Don't you ever wonder what it must have been like, traveling in those early days? You've got imagination, child—use it! The smell of dust and leather, the sound of ironbound wheels in ruts, on the road. Go on—get the *feel* of history! It's a wonderful chance. Get a sense of the past, right down in your bones, the smell of it, the taste of it."

"Well—"

"Off with you now!"

Lissa noticed that Mrs. G. never asked or suggested. She *told*. It was kind of refreshing.

And so she found herself standing in front of the village store with a group of young children waiting for the stagecoach. In a few minutes it pulled up in a cloud of dust and a jangle of harness. Jess leaped down from the driver's seat.

"Hey, there," he called to Lissa, "going to take a ride with me?"

Lissa drew herself up with dignity.

"Mrs. G. insisted—" she began.

"You can ride on top with me," he called over his shoulder as he directed the children piling into the coach.

"I'd rather ride inside."

"No more room. Come on."

She was suddenly lifted high and dumped unceremoniously on the narrow wooden driver's seat. Jess climbed up beside her.

"Want to drive?" He handed her the reins.

"Oh—no!"

She clutched the iron rail at the edge of the seat. It was awfully high up there.

"Hang on then," he said laughingly.

With a flick of the reins and a huge stomach-rocking lurch, the coach began to move.

A fine yellow dust billowed up around them, and inside the children were shouting with glee as the stagecoach rumbled down the rutted road. As they passed the yard where Barbara was working, Lissa waved.

"Your mother's been doing a great business," Jess observed. "We've never had a potter at the festival before, and every time I go by there's a crowd."

"How did you know she's my mother?" Lissa asked.

"Well, I saw you there too." Jess grinned. "Your costumes look great."

Lissa was just about to retort that they weren't costumes, when she felt a bone-cracking jolt as the coach struck a deep rut. She clung tighter to her perch.

"How do you stand this?" she gasped.

Jess chuckled.

"You just get used to it after a while. But boy, do I know what they mean when they talked about eating dust! My great-great-great-grandfather used to drive the Tuckerton Stage, so I guess it's in the blood."

"I'll take a VW any day." Lissa laughed. "But you know, this is kind of fun."

It was exciting, high up, looking down on the people who were walking at the road's edge and who waved gaily as they passed. They had to duck now and then to avoid a low-hanging tree branch. The sweating horses, the sharp scent of leather, even the dust, had a good strong smell. She could begin to imagine what life was like in those early days so long ago, raw and vital, filled with sound and color and light, not just dull history on a printed page.

"Say, this is my last run for a while," Jess' voice cut into her thoughts. "Let's go get a Coke when we get back. I'm dying of thirst."

When the coach finally drew up in front of the village store and the children were unloaded and delivered to waiting parents, Jess led Lissa to a room at the back. He drew up two packing cases in the cool gloom and from somewhere produced two frosty bottles of soda.

"How do you like Mrs. G.?" Jess asked suddenly.

"I—oh, I think she's really *neat!*" Lissa replied with enthusiasm.

"Yeah, she's kinda special," he said, taking a long swallow. "She likes you too. That's good, 'cause she doesn't like just anybody."

Lissa felt a glow of happiness begin to warm her. "I'm glad."

"You know, a lot of folks around here think—well, they think she's kinda . . . strange." Jess was looking cautious now.

"But why? I mean, she's so interesting—she knows so many things."

"Yeah, well, that's part of the reason, I guess. She's educated, for one thing. She was a teacher a long time ago."

Lissa smiled.

"I kind of figured that. Like, she's always telling you things—but in a nice way, of course."

Jess nodded. "She's still an outsider to a lot of folks. I know it sounds crazy, she's lived here for such a long time and all. But—well, you've just got to understand us Pineys." He scratched his head and smiled sheepishly. "We've been living back here in the woods for so long by ourselves, we've got our own ways. We don't take easily to strangers. People make fun of us too, outsiders—they think we're backward."

Lissa wanted to say, But *you're* not like that, and *you're* a Piney. Mrs. G. had told her that the people of the Pine Barrens could call themselves Pineys proudly but they didn't like outsiders calling them by that name.

"But Mrs. G. knows so much about the Pines, and she loves it here. You can tell, by the way she talks about it. You'd think after so many years—"

"Yeah, I know—this's a funny place."

He looked a Lissa with such genuine goodwill that she blushed.

"I'm glad you're her friend," he said simply. "And don't you pay any mind to what other folks say. She's just lonely, and she needs someone—"

He stood up suddenly and took her empty bottle.

"Hey, how about coming with me next Saturday night to hear the Pineconers?"

"Pineconers? What's that?"

"You'll see." He grinned. "A surprise. . . ."

13

On Saturday morning Lissa surveyed her clothes cupboard with mounting despair. She was particular about what she wore, and while she didn't have a lot of clothes, they were chosen with care.

She'd ruined a pair of jeans in her tumble from the bike and another pair and a shirt because of Dewey and the skunk. And here she was, with her first real date tonight—well, a kind of date, anyway—and she didn't know what to wear.

What were the Pineconers? Would it be like a concert, or a square dance, or what?

Nils and Barbara were no help at all.

"Just be comfortable and quit fussing so much," they told her.

The way her parents dressed drove Lissa wild. They just didn't seem to care how they looked—old ragged jeans and sweat shirts and work boots all the time. They were usually clean, but beyond that they looked like gypsies. It was embarrassing.

Finally, Lissa decided on the sleeveless watermelon-pink dress she'd made from an easy-to-sew pattern and her good white sandals. The dress made her look tall, but with Jess that didn't matter.

Then she began to worry.

Suppose he forgot? Maybe he won't come! I'll bet he won't even remember he asked me. She fretted. *But it might be even worse if he does come! Oh, glory! What'll I say to him?*

Lissa felt desperation rise in her.

He'll think I'm really dumb, and he'll hate me, and he'll have a rotten time, and I'll never see him again! Maybe I can have Barbara tell him I'm sick, then I won't have to go. I really do feel sick.

But then, he'll never speak to me again. Either way it'll be perfectly horrible!

At seven thirty, just about the time Lissa was reduced to total panic, a red pickup truck thundered down their lane.

"Hi!" Jess called. "Sorry we're a little late."

His father nodded in a friendly manner from the driver's seat as Jess helped Lissa into the back of the truck.

Helen-Ann was there too, sitting on a folded blanket. Lissa was partly relieved to see her, and yet at the same time she wondered if Helen-Ann was Jess' special girl. She noticed that Helen-Ann was wearing jeans and a faded plaid shirt. *Oh, dear,* she thought, *whatever it is, I'm not dressed right. Oh, I hope I can survive!*

"Dad had an emergency," Jess explained. "Some

campers let their fire get out of control. The woods are so darn dry right now—we haven't had rain for weeks."

Helen-Ann nodded.

"My dad was really mad," she said, "havin' to miss his supper."

"Everyone around here fights fire," Jess told Lissa as the truck started up and bumped down the lane. "No matter when the fire warden calls, you gotta be ready."

"Golly," Lissa's eyes were wide, "I never thought about that—fire, I mean. That's scary!"

"Yeah, a forest fire is really something. You've got to be careful, especially like now when we're on Red Alert, when everything's so dry. You see, the oaks and pines have a lot of natural resin and oil, and a few sparks can set them off. Lucky this was just a little one —they got it under control right away."

Soon the truck turned off the paved road again and plunged into a narrow sandy trail. The woods seemed to swallow them. It was like being in a tunnel, so close that they had to duck every now and then to avoid branches that swooped down on them. Occasionally another trail meandered off, immediately to lose itself in a tangle of green. It was like a maze.

"How does your dad ever find his way around back in here?" Lissa asked.

"It's part of his job," Jess replied, and then laughed. "He'd probably get lost in Brooklyn in five minutes!"

Without warning, the truck pulled into a small clearing where the twilight gloom was only a bit less than in the surrounding forest. Lissa was beginning to wonder where they were going and if this was some kind of joke being played on her, like a snipe hunt at camp.

But a dozen or so cars were parked around a little house, and a number of people were crowded by the door. From inside came the sound of music.

Jess jumped down and helped the girls.

"Looks like we can't get inside," he said. "Come on around back—let's see if we can find a window."

They made their way across a slippery carpet of pine needles to the side of the house and peered in through a patched window screen.

On one side of a small room, on plain wooden chairs drawn up in a half circle, sat three men and two women. All grizzled and well past middle age, the men wore work clothes and the women cotton-print housedresses. But this small, unlikely-looking group was whomping up a whole storm of music. The little house throbbed and rocked with the sound.

All around them, on the remaining chairs, on tables, and even on the floor, sat a crowd of people. In a corner, a bearded man was fiddling with a tape recorder.

"He's a professor, down from Rutgers," Jess whispered to Lissa. "He comes nearly every week—he's doing his thesis on folk music."

The plunkety-plunk of a banjo mingled with twanging guitars and the heavy thump of a one-string washtub bass. Together the instruments carried the weaving rhythm, while clear and strong above it a woman's voice soared.

> Beautiful, beautiful Waretown, where they
> > serve you the best beer and ale,
> We're proud of our forefathers who fought
> > at the clambake sale.
> You can live in the Forked River Mountains,
> > or down where the bay breezes blow,
> But still you're in beautiful Waretown,
> > the most wonderful place that I know.

The listeners hummed along and softly thumped their feet in time to the music.

"They make up most of their own songs," Jess said. "That's Sam Hunt on banjo, and those two old men are Joe and George Albert. This is their house. They call themselves the Pineconers."

Lissa pressed closer to the window, fascinated. This was certainly not like any concert she'd ever been to before.

"It's really different than regular country music," she whispered. "It's not so phony. It's—well, fresher and more original."

Jess seemed pleased.

"Glad you like it," he whispered back.

One guitar took the lead with a long, haunting brr-aang. The others picked it up, and the woman's voice rose once again.

> Down in the wildwood,
> > sittin' on a log,
> finger on the trigger,
> > eye on the dog,
> honey, won't you be my salty dog?
> Scaredest I was

in ever my whole life,
Uncle Ben he like to catch me
huggin' his wife!
honey, won't you be my salty dog?

Lissa, who loved folk music, was enchanted with the range and variety of the songs, some mournful tales of lost love and others racy and bawdy and full of sly fun.

"I'll bet you've been to a lot of regular concerts, big ones like the Stones an' stuff," Helen-Ann whispered to her. "This must seem kinda dinky to you."

"A few," Lissa replied, "at Madison Square Garden. I saw the Led Zeppelin there once. But this is really *neat!* It's so—different."

The concert went on for several hours. Now and then a few men would slip out of the house and congregate around one of the cars. A whiskey bottle was passed around, they'd talk quietly for a while with soft laughter and then silently go back.

Some sleepy children were bedded down on the backseat of a battered Ford, their mother returning quickly to the house so as not to miss anything.

Finally, Lissa got stiff from standing on tiptoe at the window. She walked softly to a nearby tree and sat down on a cushiony bed of moss. Overhead through the branches, stars shot shimmers of opaled fire in the night sky, and the air was tanged with pine.

Jess and Helen-Ann joined her after a while, and the three of them sat together in companionable silence as the music flowed around them like a cool spring.

14

Lissa had a sick feeling in the pit of her stomach as she walked back along the lane from the mailbox, Marcy's letter clutched in her hand.

"Oh, Barbara," she wailed, bursting into the potter's shed, "Marcy can't come!"

Her mother looked up from the whirring wheel. "Why not?"

"She's got a bad summer cold, and her mother says she's got to stay in bed."

Marcy had been invited to spend the last week of July with Lissa, and for the past two weeks the girls had been writing ecstatic letters, making plans.

"Oh, bad luck! Sorry, Lissa, I really am. Maybe she can come later."

"No, that's the awful part. Her dumb cousin is coming to her house, and she has to be there."

Lissa stalked into her own room and threw herself down on the bed.

Oh, it's just not fair! she thought miserably.

She'd never felt this lonely in her whole life. Ever since the concert, she'd been hoping to hear from Jess. She knew that he worked every day at Batsto—but still, he'd be free in the evenings. But nothing. She hadn't seen or heard from Helen-Ann either. She'd planned to take Marcy to meet them both and to visit Mrs. G. too.

Suddenly all her loneliness and all her small frustrations welled up and spilled over. Giving herself up completely to self-pity, she buried her head in the pillow and cried.

Finally, exhausted and drained, she got up and washed her face. Listlessly she looked at her bookshelves. She'd read everything there.

Well, I guess I'll have to go over to Mrs. G.'s and borrow some more books, she thought. *I'll just become the best-read person in the whole darn world, and everyone will say, "Isn't she perfectly fantastic, she knows so much." And I'll just ignore everyone because I'm so smart. Who needs people anyway?*

Mrs. G. was canning huckleberries when Lissa knocked at her door. The table was filled with clean-washed mason jars, and two large sweet-smelling kettles were simmering on the stove.

"Help yourself," she said when Lissa asked if she might borrow some books. "In there." She gestured to a door leading from the kitchen.

"I can't leave these berries just now, but you may browse around by yourself."

Lissa had never been in any part of the old black

house but the kitchen, and she admitted to a touch of curiosity as she closed the door behind her and looked around.

Two large parlors sort of flowed together to make one long room, dim and cool. They were walled with books on all four sides and crowded with ancient furniture, pictures, and statuary, all meticulously clean and seemingly in their own cluttered order.

A plaster bust of Shakespeare, aged to a creamy brown, stood by the section of shelves housing his plays, and portraits of Byron, Shelley, and Robert Frost marked the poetry shelves. The fiction was all in one section, and a tall Winged Victory of Samothrace seemed to float in the shadow of a corner collection of books on Greece.

Everywhere, piled on tables and chairs and stacked on the floor were books, books, and more books. Lissa gazed about her in pure bliss and began to browse, like a contented deer in a forest.

An hour later she was sitting on the floor examining a curious volume she'd found tucked in behind some novels. It was very old, its brown leather binding cracked and powdery and its pages brittle. The worn title, stamped in gold, read, *The Gentlewoman's Herbal,* and the date was 1843.

Exotic names leaped at her from its pages—borage, camomile, linden, asafoetida, saffron, witch hazel. It seemed to be a kind of recipe book, spiced with wise sayings.

"He who loses money loses much; he who loses a friend loses more; but he who loses his spirits loses all."

That's pretty true, Lissa pondered, thinking about her disappointment over Marcy's canceled visit. *I simply can't let myself lose my spirits, or I'm really beaten.*

Next to the saying she found a recipe for making a hair-waving solution: ". . . take one pound of quince seed in one quart of water, simmer for an hour, add a few drops of Cologne, strain, and bottle. . . ."

A few pages later she learned that Marie Antoinette's favorite bath salts were a mixture of wild thyme, marjoram, and coarse salt.

"Lissa, what on earth are you doing in there? Come, have a cup of tea."

"Oh, I just found the greatest book."

Carrying her treasure under her arm, Lissa went back to the kitchen. Beautiful jars of blue huckleberries glowed like molten sapphires on the table, and Mrs. G. was wiping her hands on a towel.

"Where did you ever get this?" Lissa asked, holding up the book.

Mrs. G. took it, riffling the pages.

"Lord! I haven't seen this for years! It belonged to my grandmother."

"It's fascinating! May I borrow it, please? I promise to take very good care of it."

"Certainly. What are you planning to do—mix up a love potion?"

Lissa looked at her in surprise.

"You mean—there'd be a recipe in here?"

"I shouldn't be surprised." Mrs. G. laughed. "Or a cure for hiccups. It's astonishing what a lot of truth and rubbish was mixed together in these old herbals. Every household had one, a hundred years ago."

"I love the sounds of the names." Lissa read. "Just listen—pennyroyal, rosemary, wintergreen, sarsparilla, sassafras—aren't they wonderful!"

"Well now, you've just given me an idea," Mrs. G. said. "How would you like to try some sassafras tea? I think I have some in the cupboard. It grows around here—many of the herbs mentioned in the book do, you know."

After a few minutes of searching, she produced a paper packet. The dark-red chips she explained were the peeled root of the sassafras tree.

"You can tell the tree by its mitten-shaped leaves," she said.

She then proceeded to steep the chips in boiling water and added a generous amount of sugar.

"It's delicious," Lissa said, tasting the rich mahogany-colored tea. "It tastes sort of—woodsy."

As she drank it, she continued to leaf through the old book.

"Here's directions for making a hand lotion. Boy, would Marcy really dig this! She was always talking about wanting to have a cosmetics company, like Helena Rubinstein or Estee Lauder or Avon, or something. She could sure get a lot of ideas from this— especially since herbal stuff is really big just now."

15

"Tell me about Marcy."

Mrs. G. poured another cup of tea for each of them and leaned back in her rocking chair.

"Well, she's my very best friend in the whole world," Lissa began.

One thing she had noticed about Mrs. G. was that she knew how to listen. A lot of people you talked to, especially grown-ups, seemed to be thinking about something else while you were talking, but not Mrs. G.

"You really miss her, don't you?" Mrs. G. said when Lissa had finished telling her all about Marcy and the things they did together.

Lissa nodded.

"It's kind of hard to explain," she was sort of thinking out loud now, "but I guess part of it is, with Marcy, it was like—well, like having a—a home, somewhere to belong. We never lived long enough in any one place for me to make a real friend."

"Yes, I can understand that. To build a real friendship, it takes time. And the best things often come slowly. Tell me about your parents."

"My parents?" Lissa was always surprised by Mrs. G.'s apparent quick change of subject. "They're—they're really neat people. I know they don't look much like parents, the way they dress and the way we live and all. Marcy always thought it was great to have folks like mine, kind of free and easy. They never tell me to do stuff all the time, you know—they're not bossy and mean. They think I ought to make my own decisions about things."

Lissa looked down at the floor. She didn't mean to be disloyal, but there was something she'd been wanting to tell someone.

"This's weird . . . I never really told anyone this before, not even Marcy. But, well, sometimes—just sometimes—I wish . . ."

She looked at Mrs. G. almost helplessly.

"Well, sometimes I wish someone would tell me what to do. I get confused about things. I wish, just for once, someone would say to me, do this, or don't do that. Is that crazy? I think part of it is that I just don't seem to belong anywhere. . . ."

Mrs. G. studied her thoughtfully.

"Life is a precarious business," she said finally. "There aren't any easy answers, Lissa."

She gestured toward the piles of books surrounding them.

"All of these came from people who were searching."

"Did any of them ever find any answers?"

"Some thought they did, for themselves at least. For

each person the answers are different. I might give you a suggestion, for what it's worth. I think it's a good idea to make the most of the moment you happen to be living, wherever you are, whomever you are with. Soak it in, absorb it, give yourself to a place or a person completely.

"Think about it."

She smiled at Lissa.

"Meanwhile, books are good companions for your journey, but I think you already know that. If you have a good book, you're never really alone. And remember, there's a vast difference between being lonely and being alone."

Lissa returned her smile with a sudden surge of warmth.

"You know what?" she cried impulsively. "I wish you were my grandmother!"

Mrs. G.'s face closed suddenly. It was as if a mask had dropped over it. Her eyes grew distant.

"Well, I'm not," she snapped. "I'm nobody's grand-mother, nor do I have any wish to be."

She stood up abruptly.

"Now you'd best be getting along home. Take the book with you if you like."

As Lissa pedaled her bike down the road a few minutes later, she was busy thinking, puzzled by Mrs. G.'s sudden coldness.

Wow—what did I say wrong?

She darn near threw me out of the house!

Why?

Grown-ups are certainly hard to figure out. All I said

was about wishing she was my grandmother. That's what did it! Could it be—I wonder . . .

I wonder, she thought with a sudden flash of insight, *is Mrs. G. shy, too? Afraid to let herself care for anyone, for fear she'll get hurt? Did she give advice to me that she's afraid to take herself?*

It was hard to imagine that a grown-up could be shy.

I must try to find out more about her, about the daughter she never talks about. I have to write to Marcy about this. Oh, and tell her about the herbal, too.

And then a fantastic idea struck her!

When Lissa arrived home, she found Nils busy at the typewriter. He'd finally begun his book, and she didn't like to bother him with her exciting plan. When she stuck her head in the door of the potter's shed, Barbara was bent over her wheel, concentrating on a new and intricate piece. She didn't even look up.

"Barbara, do we have any thyme or marjoram?"

"I think so—in the spice rack."

Lissa found the herbs, and since she knew they didn't have any coarse salt, she took a box of regular salt and disappeared into the bathroom.

The water in the tub looked kind of gray-green and icky when she'd sprinkled in the herbs, but it smelled strangely fragrant, and she took off her clothes and slipped into its delicious coolness. July in the Pine Barrens could be murderously hot.

She lay back in the tub, listening to the clickety-clack of Nils' typewriter and the faraway hum of the potter's wheel. The subtle scent of the herbal water was soothing and delightful.

Why not? she thought dreamily. *I can gather the herbs in the woods and blend them. Marcy can handle the business part of it in New York, the selling and stuff. We can use the old-fashioned recipes from* The Gentlewoman's Herbal. *We can start our own cosmetics company!*

"Lissa, have you died in there?"

Nils was pounding at the bathroom door.

"Hey, come on—give a guy a chance, will you!"

Lissa roused herself slowly.

"What? Oh, sorry—I'll be right out. Hey, Nils— I've just had the most fabulous idea!"

AUGUST

16

For the next two weeks, Lissa made excursions into the woods by herself every day, going a little farther each time. She'd made a list of the herbs she wanted to find, and she'd remembered reading somewhere how the pioneers blazed trails by cutting notches on trees. She used this method for finding her way home again, for the woods were still wild and bewildering to her.

Nils had bought her a paperback book on trees and shrubs, and with this, an old pair of pruning shears, a trowel, and a basket, she planned to forage for the plants she needed.

At first it was hard. A growing plant looked different from the illustrations on the pages of a book. Walking slowly, with her eyes on the ground, she was soon amazed at the diversity of wild flowers and plants that grew in the forest, shy, hidden things that a casual glance would miss. It was exciting to find one that she recognized, like seeing a familiar face in a crowd of strangers.

Huckleberry was everywhere, but the wild thyme took some hunting. She found teaberry, wintergreen, and wild indigo in abundance and gathered them for later use and experiment. The herbal had many recipes she was anxious to try. There was a lot of the matlike sphagnum moss, which she learned had many wonderful properties. It was even used by soldiers during the Revolution as a substitute for bandages.

During her lonely rambles, Lissa began to notice other things too. Bluejays stitched threads of brilliant blue through the trees, exquisite in their suddenness, and then gone. Quick, unexpected flashes of movement—the brush of a squirrel's tail vanishing behind a tree limb, a darting dragonfly—these no longer startled her.

She noticed the nutlike droppings of rabbits and the gnawed remnants of acorns where squirrels had feasted on the forest floor, stripped branches where deer had fed and their deep-bitten footprints at the edges of streams. Everywhere around her a secret life was humming and throbbing, and she felt a growing joy in it.

She was not a part of it yet, not really. But she knew, deep inside and without words, that her own life here in the Pines was beginning somehow.

Meanwhile, her collection of herbs was growing. She tied them in small bunches to dry and hung them from a rope stretched across the ceiling of her bedroom. Their scent filled the air, and at night when she went to sleep, she was enfolded in their fragrance.

Lissa was beginning to feel a new kind of excitement, different from any she'd ever known before. She could hardly wait to get up in the morning and be off again for another day's exploring.

Now that she was learning to recognize certain plants, she was eager to find new ones. She was looking at things more carefully, beginning to notice, for example, the many different shades of green. It was amazing how many variations there were to one color —blue-green of juniper, yellow green of Scotch pine, almost-black of cedar, emerald of moss.

One afternoon Lissa was sitting on the bank of a small pond she'd discovered. It lay back of Mrs. G.'s cranberry bogs, glowing in lonely splendor, reflecting sky and forest fringe. She was watching five wild swans floating like a string of pearls on the quiet water.

Suddenly she became aware of a moving shadow. She heard the crunch of boots on gravel. Startled, she looked up to see Jess standing there. It was the first time she'd seen him since the night of the Pineconers' concert.

He put his finger to his lips and hunkered down beside her.

"They must have come in last night," he whispered. "I've been waiting for them. They come every year."

Lissa didn't speak. Together they watched until finally the great graceful birds moved to the far end of the pond. There they began to feed in the shallows, dipping their sinuous necks beneath the water like white sickles harvesting the water grasses.

Jess leaned back.

"Aren't they something!"

Lissa finally spoke, in a whisper.

"I never saw anything so beautiful."

"They're mute swans," he told her. "They can't make a sound, like the trumpeter swans. You can tell them by the bright orange bill. I guess maybe that's why I like them so much—they're quiet."

He looked at her curiously.

"What're you doing way back here?"

"Oh, just exploring."

Lissa had no intention of telling him about collecting herbs. He'd probably think it was silly.

He laughed suddenly.

"All by yourself? Aren't you afraid the Jersey Devil'll get you?"

Something in his tone of voice made her bristle.

"I can take care of myself," she said haughtily.

"Well, for a city kid I guess you're not too bad."

"Gee, thanks," she retorted with sarcasm, and added, "And just what's wrong with 'city kids'?"

He flushed slightly.

"Oh . . . you know—they always think they're so darn smart. You ought to see some of the weirdos my dad meets up with—think they're big hotshot woodsmen. Hah!"

He hooted in derision.

Lissa stood up and began to gather up her book and basket.

"Sounds to me like you feel pretty hotshot yourself," she snapped. "You people who live here sure won't give any outsider even half a chance—"

"Hey—what did I say wrong?"

"Oh, nothing. Forget it."

Without a backward glance, she started down the sandy trail beside the bog.

"Hey—wait a minute."

Jess was running to catch up with her.

"I'm sorry—honest. I didn't mean to sound superior. I sure don't feel it!"

Lissa continued walking in silence. She was feeling stupid and ashamed of herself. She knew he hadn't been deliberately making fun of her. She had just come to this new realization of confidence in herself, for almost the first time in her life. But to Jess she was still just another 'city kid.' Well, he'd ignored her for two weeks, and she didn't need him now.

He was half hopping along beside her.

"It's just that—well, I guess I don't understand girls very much."

He rubbed his head in a funny, awkward manner, and his voice trailed off.

Lissa stopped suddenly and turned to him.

"It's okay," she said. "And I didn't mean to be rude." She grinned at him.

"I don't understand boys very much either. Heck, I don't even understand myself sometimes. . . ."

"I just never knew a girl like you before," he said with great seriousness. "You're so—different. The clothes you wear, the way you look—"

Lissa bristled again. "What's wrong with the way I look?"

"Oh, for crying out loud—nothing!" His tone was exasperated now. "What I'm trying to say is—well, I *like* the way you look!"

Lissa stared at him in astonishment.

"I'm too tall."

"No, you're not. And anyway, I like tall girls."

"You do? Honest?"

She straightened a bit.

"I always feel like I'm sticking out a mile, or something. Everywhere I go I'm always looking down at people. It's dismal."

"You can't look down at me," he laughed.

"No, I guess I can't," she admitted.

He stuck out his hand.

"Friends."

She grasped it.

"Okay," she said, "friends."

They began to walk again, side by side.

17

Stopping at the mailbox on her way to the store the next morning, Lissa was delighted to find a letter from Marcy. She sat down on a tussock of grass at the road's edge to read it immediately.

Marcy was enthused about the idea of the herbal bath salts and full of plans for selling them to the kids of the neighborhood. But the end of her letter gave Lissa a small gnawing uneasiness.

". . . a new girl moved in next door—she's really neat, from Puerto Rico—her dad's an architect . . . she's teaching me Spanish . . . adios mi amiga!"

Lissa folded it slowly and stuck it in her pocket. She ought to be glad. When she went to New York, they'd be three instead of two. *What's wrong with that?* she asked herself. *Marcy'll still be* my *friend first.* But some edge of brightness had gone unexplainably from the day.

When Lissa walked into Simpkins' Store, Helen-Ann

was there, studying a shelf of shampoo. Lissa hadn't seen her either since the night of the concert.

"Hi," she called, and walked over to join her.

"Oh, hi, Lissa," Helen-Ann said shyly, and nodded. "I was wondering . . . what kind of shampoo do you use?"

"This's a good one." Lissa selected a bottle from the shelf.

"Okay, I'll try it. My hair's so oily, it never looks good. Maybe this'll help."

"And try brushing a lot too. At first it seems to make your hair more oily, but in a little while it really does look better."

Discussing hair problems, the girls made their purchases. Then, on an impulse, Lissa said, "How about an ice-cream bar? I'll treat."

"Gee, thanks."

They walked out of the store together and sat down on the stone wall at the edge of the bridge to eat their ice cream. The river rippled silver-slate in the morning sun, its layered light sheening on the underside of the bridge. Around them the quiet town dreamed the morning away.

"This must be a nice place to live," Lissa said, looking about at the clustered houses beneath their sheltering trees.

"Yeah—it's okay, I guess," Helen-Ann replied, licking chocolate from her fingers. "I'll bet it seems pretty dinky to you though, after New York City."

"It's different, of course. But it must be neat, knowing everyone, and well . . . belonging someplace."

"I never thought about it that way. Sometimes it would be nice to see someone besides your own cousins. Golly, it seems like everyone in town is related, and everyone always knows all your business. I mean—they just take you for granted."

Lissa looked at her in surprise.

"I never thought about it that way."

"Well, it's true," Helen-Ann replied with some heat. "I'm just fat old Helen-Ann Sprague."

"But—"

"Yeah," she continued bitterly, "an' dumb. I'm not smart like the Cowperthwaites—"

"Wait a minute!" Lissa cried. "You're just as good as anyone! Don't run yourself down."

"Look at me—I'm a mess," Helen-Ann rushed on. "I eat too much, an' I got pimples, an'—"

"Hold it!" Lissa interrupted. "There's nothing you can't change, if you really want to. Look, if you'd like, I'll help—I mean, if you want to go on a diet, why I'll yell at you if you don't stick to it, and I'll weigh you and keep a record—stuff like that."

"Would you? Honest?"

"Sure. And we can make you some new clothes, too. I've got a sewing machine. I'm not too great, but I can do the easy-to-sew stuff."

Just then a shrill voice from the house across the street sliced the morning stillness.

"Helen-Ann—Helen-Ann . . ."

"Oh, darn—that's my mom. I gotta baby-sit while

she goes to the doctor."

"I'll see you soon." Lissa waved after her retreating figure. "And try that shampoo for starters."

As Lissa got on her bike, she was thinking about Helen-Ann. She really seemed to need a friend. It was a puzzling thought. It was hard to imagine someone who had lived all her life in one place, surrounded by relatives, who could be lonely too. She wasn't as glamorous as a girl who spoke Spanish, but—*Well, maybe I can find a new friend too,* she thought.

But Lissa was feeling lonely again, and strangely out of sorts. She didn't feel like going back to the cabin, and she decided to bike down the river road for a while.

She rode past a few houses facing the river and some summer cottages, and then, farther on down, she could see that the road ended. An old abandoned cedar-shingle house stood almost at the road's end. It looked like Mrs. G.'s house, only smaller. Its broken windows and sagging door gaped like black holes. A straggle of wild rose and lilac seemed to be all that was holding it upright. Back beyond was a small white frame church with a graveyard beside it.

Lissa leaned her bike against a tree and went over to examine some of the weathered gravestones. Ancient and wind-worn, grayed with time and lichen, they leaned at crazy angles.

It wasn't a scary place. It was sad, and peaceful too. The only sound was the sleepy thrum of a bee in the tall grasses. Lissa knelt and ran her fingers lightly over one of the tilted stones.

James Cowperthwaite
son of
William and Martha
Born April 3, 1845
Wounded at Cold Harbour
June 6, 1864
died
November 18, 1864
Requiescat in Pace

Lissa let out her breath softly. This must have been one of Jess' ancestors. The Civil War! James Cowperthwaite was only nineteen when he died—just a few years older than Jess is now. Probably it was his first battle, and he was wounded and brought home to die.

He lay surrounded by other Cowperthwaites—Henry George was ninety-seven when he died in 1876. A little one, Hepzibah, died in 1803, aged three years and seven months. A tiny weathered stone lamb with a chipped ear marked her small grave.

There were Spragues and Cavileers and Johnsons—all names that Lissa had seen on the mailboxes in town.

She rocked back on her heels.

Despite what Helen-Ann had said, this was what she was looking for—this feeling of permanence. It must be wonderful to belong somewhere. There had always been Spragues and Cowperthwaites here, and there always would be.

She stood up thoughtfully and gazed back at the graveyard and then ahead to the clustered roofs of the town. In a curious way, this must be what it was like to really have a home.

18

"Barbara, I need help," Lissa confided to her mother. "Could you please make me some little clay pots, about so high?"

She cupped her hands to show the size she wanted. "What for?"

"Remember, I told you about the herbal bath salts I'm making from the recipe in that old book? I think they'd look nice in some pretty containers, something unusual. Marcy wrote that she'd try to sell some of it to the kids on the block."

"That sounds like a marvelous idea. How many do you want?"

"About a dozen, to start with. Gee, Barbara, I'd really appreciate it. . . ."

Lissa spent the afternoon at her desk trying to design a label. She discarded quite a number before she finally decided on one. She and Marcy had decided to call their products Forest House—it sounded properly woodsy—and though she wasn't much of an artist, she managed a simple sketch of a tiny log cabin with a spray of pine above it, tinted delicately with watercolor.

Delighted with the result, she hurriedly put it in the mail to Marcy. In her letter she made no mention of the new girl.

By the end of the week, the pots were finished. Made of rough terra-cotta with tiny lids, they looked handsome when she pasted on the labels she had painted. She crumbled her dried herbs and measured them carefully according to the directions in *The Gentlewoman's Herbal*. As a finishing touch she tied a narrow moss-green ribbon around each pot.

Even Nils was impressed. He'd been out all week, having discovered a man who carved duck decoys and spending hours watching and talking to him, and he had missed all of the activity at home.

He surveyed the row of pots on the table.

"They're just great!" he cried, giving Lissa an enormous bear hug. *"Min elskling,* you're a wonder!"

Lissa hugged him back.

"I'm really proud of them," she crowed. "I never expected they'd look so good. Now, we have to find a big box to pack them in so we can mail them to Marcy."

"Maybe we'll even get rich," Nils said as he helped Lissa wrap the pots. "Then I can really retire."

Suddenly he straightened up.

"Hey, Barb," he called. "I just had a great idea. Why don't we take these up to the city, instead of mailing them? You could do with a little vacation. And you've made a lot more pots since the Crafts Festival. We could try to sell them to some of the shops in Greenwich Village."

Lissa's heart leaped.

"Oh, Nils! That'd be wonderful!" she cried. "Then I could get to see Marcy."

She felt a special need, an urgency, to go back now. She wouldn't admit it, even to herself, not in words anyway, but it was there—go back before it's too late.

Barbara nodded happily.

"I'd love to get out of the woods for a while, Nils. And I really do have a lot of stuff made—it's just piling up. And boy, the extra money would come in handy, too, if I can sell them."

Lissa could hardly contain her delight. She grabbed Dewey's front paws and danced him around the room.

"We're going to New Yo-ork . . . we're going to New Yo-ork. . . ."

Dewey didn't understand what all the excitement was about, but he wagged his tail and barked joyfully.

Lissa could hardly wait to see Marcy's face when she would show her the Forest House bath salts. And she had so much to tell her she felt she would just fly apart in a thousand pieces.

Nils brought in a lot of cardboard cartons, and the three of them spent the whole evening packing the pottery. There really was an awful lot of it!

"I just didn't have anything else to do," Barbara laughed almost apologetically.

It was dark before Nils began to load the little VW with the cartons. Lissa was in her room, humming to herself and packing her overnight case, trying to decide what to wear and what to pack. She looked up to see

Nils standing in the doorway. He came in and sat down on the edge of her bed.

"Min elskling," he said softly. "I don't know how to tell you this . . ."

He pulled at his red beard.

"I'm afraid there won't be room for you to go."

Lissa looked at him in disbelief.

"Oh—no!"

Her heart plummeted to her stomach with a dreadful flop.

"You're kidding me."

"Look, *min elskling*—a VW only holds so much. It doesn't have elastic sides, and it's packed to the roof now."

"But—couldn't we leave some of the cartons? I won't take up much room—I'll scrunch up—"

"If we're going to make the trip pay, we've got to take all of it. We could sure use the extra money, Lissa. It's costing more than we figured, living here. And with food prices going up—well, the truth is we really need to sell that pottery."

"Oh, Nils! It's just not fair! I was counting on—"

"Barbara offered to stay here, so you could go," Nils said, "but it's important that she talk directly with the buyers herself, and make the contacts."

He stood up to leave.

"You can get that girl—what's her name? Helen-Ann?—to stay with you. It's only for one night. And you'll have fun. How about it?"

Lissa looked at her father resentfully.

"But I don't even know her that well. And anyway—"

"Well, we can ask her." Nils' tone had already settled the matter. "And I promise, solemn word of honor, that I'll take you up to New York before school starts. . . ."

19

The next morning they drove over to Helen-Ann's house, and Nils made arrangements with her mother for Helen-Ann to stay over at the cabin the next night. Lissa pouted in the car and waited for him. She knew she was acting childish, but she didn't care.

It wasn't fair of them to go without her, and she wasn't going to pretend to be happy about it. She hadn't told them about Marcy's letter, about how important it was to see her now, to reassure herself that they were still best friends. Her parents wouldn't understand anyway.

Sometimes I just don't like Nils and Barbara very much, she thought angrily. *They're not mean, but they sure are thoughtless. They just don't care how I feel.*

Helen-Ann came out to the car with Nils.

"I can hardly wait," she whispered excitedly to Lissa. "I'll come over to your place on my bike tomorrow morning. It'll be fun!"

Lissa tried to manage a half-hearted smile.

Their next stop was Simpkins' Store. Again Lissa just sat in the car while Nils went in to buy frozen pizza, Coke, potato chips, and a lot of other stuff he thought the girls would like. He returned carrying three large bags.

"We have to make another stop," he told Lissa, "to deliver a bag of groceries to Mrs. G. She always phones in her order, but Mr. Simpkins is out with the truck, so I told Aunt Sally we'd drop this off on our way home."

When they stopped at Mrs. G.'s house, Nils asked Lissa to carry in the bag of groceries. She went around to the back door, and at first there was no answer to her knock. Then she heard, faintly, from inside the kitchen a voice calling.

"Come in—the door's unlocked."

Mrs. G. was sitting in her rocking chair by the table. One foot was propped up on a stool. A look of surprise crossed her face when she saw Lissa.

"Oho! So Simpkins have a new delivery girl?"

Lissa smiled and explained.

"What happened to you?" she asked.

"I turned my ankle coming down the stairs this morning," Mrs. G. said. "Just a sprain, nothing serious. But I find that walking is a bit more than I can manage today. I'll be spry as a sparrow in a day or two."

"Is there anything I can do for you?"

"Well, now that you're here, could you brew me a cup of tea? If your father won't mind waiting for a few minutes."

As far as I'm concerned, he can wait all day, Lissa was about to say, but she held her tongue.

She fixed a pot of tea for Mrs. G. and arranged fruit and cheese and crackers on the table within easy reach. And she also fixed a dish of cat food for the still-invisible Oliver.

"Now we're all set for the day," Mrs. G. said. "Thank you, Lissa."

"I'll check on you tomorrow."

"No need." Mrs. G.'s tone was sharp. "I'll be fine. Now scurry. . . ."

Dawn the next morning was just an apricot smudge in the eastern sky when Nils and Barbara left for New York.

Barbara hugged her daughter.

"I'm really sorry, honey," she whispered. "I know how much it meant to you. But we'll make it up to you, honest."

Lissa and Dewey stood forlornly on the cabin step as the VW started down the lane.

"Now don't forget," Barbara called. "You can always go over to Mrs. G.'s in case of an emergency."

"Have fun, *min elskling*," Nils shouted, and waved from the car window. "See you tomorrow night."

20

"What a super place!" Helen-Ann cried enthusiastically.

She was standing in the center of the living room, clutching a brown paper bag containing her pajamas and toothbrush.

"I never saw so many books and pretty things!"

Lissa looked at her bleakly.

"You can have Nils and Barbara's room. I only have a single bed. Come on, you can put your stuff in here."

She stamped across the room. She'd much rather have enjoyed her misery alone, but now that Helen-Ann was here, she knew she'd have to try to be a little bit gracious.

"Wow! A whole room to myself!"

Helen-Ann was awed. She held up the paper bag.

"I really feel dumb. I don't even have a suitcase. I never stayed over before, except at my grandma's, an' that doesn't count."

Helen-Ann certainly was easy to please. She didn't

seem to notice Lissa's bad humor, and she was curious about everything in the cabin.

"What're those?" she asked, pointing to the herbs drying in Lissa's room.

Lissa told her about the herbal bath salts and showed her the pots she'd kept for herself.

"I never heard of anything like that before. They're gorgeous!"

Lissa let her look at *The Gentlewoman's Herbal.* Helen-Ann riffled through the pages with interest.

"Hey, listen to this—'. . . botanicals that cause a distaste for tobacco, taken as an in—infusion.' What's an infusion?"

"Mrs. G. told me that it's a mixture of herbs steeped in boiling water," Lissa explained.

"It says," Helen-Ann read on, " '. . . take a mixture of wild oats, huckleberry, ribwort plantain, and camomile. . . . ' " She looked at Lissa, "Do you think it works?"

"I don't know. I never mixed that one. Why?"

"Well, I smoke too much," Helen-Ann confided. "Do you smoke?"

"No," Lissa replied, then added, in case Helen-Ann might think she was childish, "I mean, I tried it a couple of times, but I didn't really like it."

"I started about a year ago," Helen-Ann said, pulling a pack of cigarettes from her pocket. "My mom'd kill me if she knew. All the kids at school were doing it, you know. But I really would like to quit, because of cancer and stuff. Maybe I could try this, huh?"

Lissa read the recipe again.

"Sounds horrible. I do have all the herbs though, except the wild oats. Maybe rolled oats, cereal you know, would work."

"Let's try it," Helen-Ann said.

"Okay—if you really want to."

They spent the rest of the morning in the kitchen, measuring, stewing, and straining the foul-smelling mixture.

"Yeccch." Helen-Ann wrinkled her nose. "I'm not sure I want to quit smoking that much."

"We'll let it cool first, anyway," Lissa laughed. "Maybe if it's chilled it won't taste too bad. You can try it later."

Helen-Ann leaned against the sink and lit a cigarette.

"One last fling," she said. "Want one?"

"Sure, why not?" Lissa replied.

She found it wasn't too bad if she didn't try to inhale.

They decided to have a picnic, so they packed a huge lunch. Lissa was feeling more cheerful as they carried their basket deep into the woods, Dewey trotting along behind them.

After they ate they each smoked another cigarette, lying back on the soft moss under the trees. *Maybe if I get cancer and die, then Nils and Barbara will be sorry,* Lissa thought. *Then they'll wish they'd cared more about me.*

It was nearly suppertime when they returned to the cabin, grubby and tired from roaming in the woods. Lissa was surprised to discover that she actually knew more about the forest then Helen-Ann did. She'd

115

showed her many things, and they'd gathered wild huckleberries, stuffing themselves until their lips were blue.

"Gee," Helen-Ann said in admiration. "You know almost as much about the woods as Jess Cowperthwaite."

"Not that much—but I'm learning," Lissa laughed.

Lissa let Helen-Ann soak in a cool tub of herbal bath salts while she fixed dinner. As she put the pizza into the oven and cut up fresh fruit for a salad, she could hear Helen-Ann splashing and humming contentedly. A sudden thought struck her.

She'd really been having a pretty good time!

Helen-Ann wasn't as exciting or imaginative as Marcy, but it was a novel experience to be admired. It was obvious that Helen-Ann thought everything Lissa did was special.

She was impressed with Lissa's room.

"I have to share a room with my two creepy sisters," she'd confided.

And she thought Lissa's clothes were spectacular.

"You always look just fabulous," she'd remarked wistfully, and Lissa had promised to help her make a new pantsuit for school.

Maybe this isn't going to be such a bad year after all, Lissa thought. For the first time in her life she had a friend who seemed to need *her.*

After supper the girls washed the dishes and then began to play a game of Monopoly.

"I'm sorry we don't have television," Lissa apologized as she stacked records on the stereo. "My folks don't believe in it."

"No kidding! I never heard of anyone without TV."

"I know, it's weird. But they think it's a big waste of time. We don't even have a telephone."

"Well, you can come over to my house anytime, to watch TV. I love *The Waltons*—come over for that. Hey, we can really stay up late tonight, huh? Isn't it neat—not having grown-ups around! We can do just what we feel like doing."

When Helen-Ann landed on Lissa's Park Place with two hotels, the game was over.

"Let's fix a snack," Lissa suggested. "You can start on your diet tomorrow."

They made two great, gooey banana splits in soup bowls, giggling as they squirted whipped cream at each other.

Just then Helen-Ann noticed the bottle of herbal infusion sitting on the windowsill.

"Golly, I forgot all about it. Do you think I ought to try some?"

"Sure—why the heck not?" Lissa laughed. "Put it in some Coke, then it won't taste so bad."

She mixed about a half a cup of the infusion into a tall glass of Coke and ice and handed it to Helen-Ann.

Helen-Ann took a tentative sip and made a face.

"Go on, drink it down," Lissa urged. "You'll never know if you don't try it."

"Well—okay." And she swallowed the whole glassful.

"How do you feel?" Lissa asked.

"All right. It really wasn't all that bad. I just feel like

I ate too much, though."

By now they were both yawning, exhausted by their long day.

"Let's turn in," Lissa said.

It was fun, calling good night between their rooms. And Lissa fell asleep feeling happier than she'd been in a long time.

21

"Lissa! Lissa! Wake up!"

Lissa felt rough hands shaking her. Dazed with sleep, she rubbed her eyes.

"Wha—what—"

Helen-Ann's face, deathly pale in the glaring electric light, leaned over her.

"We've got to get out—the woods are on fire!"

Still drugged with sleep, Lissa couldn't force her mind to work properly.

"What time is it?"

"I don't know—what difference does it make?" Helen-Ann's voice was frantic. "Oh, come on—*hurry!*"

Lissa reached for her robe and slippers. She was aware of Dewey barking somewhere. Stumbling, she followed Helen-Ann to the front door of the cabin.

Then with a flash she came fully awake!

Through the open door she could see flames springing in the woods beyond, licking at the sky with a hundred long orange fingers. She heard an ominous crackle.

She spun around, her eyes wide with terror.

"What'll we do?"

"Run as fast as we can for the road!" Helen-Ann cried.

Lissa felt as if her legs were made of lead.

"I c—c—can't."

She stared as if hypnotized by the blazing trees all around the cabin.

"We've got to—it's our only chance." Helen-Ann began to pull her through the door.

Lissa felt herself go limp. Without protest she allowed herself to be dragged along, making no resistance.

Outside, the woods were like a rippling wall of flame. A blast of searing air made her shrink back.

"If we can get to the road, we'll have a chance," Helen-Ann shouted. "Come on—run!"

Lissa turned.

"Dewey—"

"He'll follow us. Oh, for God's sake—*hurry!*"

Ahead of them the lane seemed to be open. The fire eerily lighted their way as they pounded over the slippery dry carpet of pine's needles.

Lissa's heart raced in time with her flying feet. Her breath came in hurtful gasps.

"I—c—can't run any faster."

"You gotta! It's not far now."

Stumbling and panting, they reached the paved road. It gleamed dull gold in the flickering light. Only when they reached it did Helen-Ann finally let go of Lissa's hand.

Lissa sank to her knees on the road, burying her head in her hands. Every breath she took was agony. Finally the stitch in her side eased a bit. She looked up at Helen-Ann, her teeth chattering.

"I'm—s—so—scared."

Helen-Ann's face was chalky even in the golden fire-light.

"We gotta get outa here . . ." she kept saying.

With one accord, they began to run again, heading down the road in the general direction of town.

To their right the wall of flaming trees rose hideously higher. On the other side the dark forest loomed hushed—tense and waiting.

When they could no longer run they walked at a jog-trot, not speaking, saving every ounce of breath. So after what seemed an endless time, alternately running and walking, they outdistanced the fire a bit.

Lissa, tripping over her own feet, fell heavily in the middle of the road.

"I can't go on," she gasped. "I've got to rest a minute."

Helen-Ann dropped in exhaustion beside her. Crawling to her side, panting, Dewey laid his head in her lap.

Behind them the pines at the edge of the road loomed black and skeletal against a glowing screen of fire. The sky overhead glowed an angry red-orange, smudged with billowing smoke. Around them the air hissed and crackled.

The fire, having reached the open space of the road, was now backtracking, fanning out on either side. It writhed its way hungrily through the glistening oils of the resinous wood, leaping from dry ground cover of pine needles upward through the smaller oaks to the taller pines.

"Someone's sure to have seen it by now," Helen-Ann half sobbed. "Oh—why doesn't someone come!"

The empty road taunted them, undulating in the fiery light.

With great effort Lissa struggled to her feet. She pulled at Helen-Ann, who was still gasping for breath.

"We've got to keep going."

Once more they began to run.

Now the fire seemed to be moving eastward, following them, driven by a wind that had maliciously sprung up and whipped savagely at their backs.

There was a terrible rushing sound too. Hooting and howling, it sounded as if a giant railroad train was bearing down on them. It was the burning forest roaring its agony, a sound Lissa would never forget.

They covered another mile at a jog trot. Running in silence to conserve strength, they did not dare to look behind them.

Lissa stopped so suddenly that Helen-Ann crashed into her.

"What!"

"Mrs. G.!"

Helen-Ann looked at her blankly.

"She hurt her foot, and she can't walk."

Lissa felt something like a giant fist close about her heart.

"We've got to get to her."

Lissa pointed to the direction in which the fire was moving.

"See—it *is* heading toward her place—oh, we've got to hurry!"

"But it's too dangerous—" Helen-Ann began to object.

Lissa pulled at her arm impatiently.

"It's only about half a mile—come on!"

Strength born of fear surged through her.

"We've got to help her."

The regular *thock* of their thudding feet hitting the empty road beat an even tattoo. *I wonder,* Lissa thought crazily, *if this is what hell is like?* Every jarring step hurt, every breath was a rasping pain. The flames roaring and screaming, biting chunks out of the night with sharp yellow teeth. . . .

At last, sodden with sweat, they reached the old black house at the corner of the two roads.

For the rest of her life, Lissa would always have that scene imprinted indelibly on her memory.

The house with its pointed gables looked like an etching scratched finely on bronze. Behind it flame shimmered like a silken curtain of orange-gold, rippling and swaying in deep folds. Every line of roof, window, and door lintel stood cleanly outlined in the fierce light, though by now a grainy wind was showering them with powdered ash.

On the porch a monstrous crooked shadow figure crawled on hands and knees.

It was like a scene from Edgar Allan Poe.

Lissa halted.

Behind her, Helen-Ann drew in her breath sharply. She clutched at Lissa's hand, her face contorted with fear.

"I'm —s—scared," Helen-Ann stuttered.

I can't, Lissa thought suddenly. *I can't go toward that fire.*

She threw one anguished look at the crablike figure crawling on the porch.

Then she began to run.

22

Lissa could hear Helen-Ann's footsteps behind her.

"We're coming," she called to Mrs. G.

The old woman had reached the porch steps when they came running up the path. Lissa could see that the house itself had not yet begun to burn, though the woods behind it were a mass of flame.

"Bless you," Mrs. G. murmured brokenly.

Far in the distance they could hear the eerie wail of sirens rising and falling above the crackling of the fire.

"If you could just lend me a shoulder to lean on, I think I can walk," Mrs. G. said.

She used the porch post for a support and painfully hauled herself upright.

"We can carry you," Lissa said.

Somewhere, in all of her random reading, she remembered how two people could make a hand seat to transport an injured person. Quickly she explained to Helen-Ann how, by grasping your own wrist with one hand and another person's wrist with the other, a kind of firm swinglike seat could be made.

Dewey, exhausted by fright and his long run, lay panting on the steps. Mrs. G. glanced at him.

"Oliver—"

"Is he still in the house?"

"I think so—probably under my bed."

Lissa drew in a deep breath.

"I'll see if I can find him."

Helen-Ann looked at her in astonishment.

"Oh, Lissa, we don't have time."

"It'll just take a minute." She was running into the house.

"Lissa," Mrs. G. called, "if you can't find him immediately, just leave the door open—he'll have to take his own chances. . . ."

The familiar rooms glimmered strangely in the angry red light from the fire outside, like the haunted house in an amusement park. In her haste Lissa tripped over a chair. Picking herself up and swearing softly, she raced upstairs to the bedroom.

Fortunately, the electricity was still on, and she snapped on the overhead light. She threw herself on the floor and peered under the bed. Two enormous glowing green eyes flashed at her.

"Here, kitty—kitty . . ."

She began to wiggle under the bed toward the far corner where the suspicious cat crouched.

She reached for him. Suddenly a paw slashed.

"Ouch! Damn you!"

She pulled her arm back, raked and bleeding. Oliver, his back a perfect arc, hissed her a warning.

"I'll fix you," she muttered, determined now.

Inching out from under the bed, she snatched up a pillowcase.

"Lissa! Lissa!" She could hear her name being called urgently.

"Come on, Oliver." She tried to keep her voice low and coaxing. "I won't hurt you—come on, kitty."

It was hard to pounce, flattened under the bed, but Lissa managed. She flung the open end of the pillowcase over the frightened cat.

Dragging her wiggling burden behind her, Lissa crawled out from under the bed. She hurried downstairs and raced onto the porch.

"Oh, child, you shouldn't have—" Mrs. G. began.

Lissa thrust the thrashing pillowcase into Mrs. G.'s arms.

"Well, I finally saw Oliver," she snapped, "and I don't think much of him!"

Quickly she and Helen-Ann grasped each other's wrists to make a seat. Mr. G. positioned herself between them, one arm about Lissa's neck and the other holding the yowling cat.

They knew that their burden made it impossible to run, but they began to walk as fast as possible. The old lady was surprisingly frail and light, and by the time they reached the road again, they had synchronized their steps. They found that they were able to move at a fairly comfortable jog. No one spoke, nor did they once look back.

They had not gone far down the road before they saw headlights approaching. A truck slowed down as it picked them up in its blinding beams. It pulled to a

stop beside them, and a man leaned out of the cab.

"You folks need help?"

Lissa could see that the truck carried hoses and a large water tank. The driver recognized Mrs. G.

"Hey, it's Mrs. Gilfillan. You okay?"

"Oh—Barney! Yes, I'm all right."

"Your home caught?"

"I don't think so—not yet anyway. I think we can make it to town."

"Okay, if you're sure. There'll be more trucks along in a few minutes. We'll try to save your house."

With a jangle of gears the truck lumbered off.

Already they could see more headlights slicing the darkness. A battered old station wagon stopped beside them.

"Hop in. I'll run you into town."

The old man driving was Fred Simpkins, the husband of Aunt Sally who kept the store.

"Lucky you was able to git out," he remarked as they climbed in, settling Mrs. G. carefully on the front seat. "Looks like this is gonna be a ringer."

He turned the station wagon around and headed back toward town.

"Anywhere's you'd like to go?" he queried. "You're welcome to our place."

"I gotta get home," Helen-Ann murmured. "My mom'll be worried sick."

She glanced at Lissa.

"You wanna come with me?"

"Thank you, Fred," Mrs. G. replied before Lissa could answer. "If you'll just take Lissa and me to the Cowperthwaites—I think they'll have room to take us in temporarily."

Lissa clutched Dewey, who lay in her lap. In her present state of shock she simply couldn't think. She stared with glazed eyes at the stream of cars now hurtling down the road and heard the wail of sirens rising and falling through the night.

In a few minutes the station wagon lurched to a stop in front of a big white house with two huge sycamore trees by the front door. Light blazed from every window.

"Hang on a minute," Fred instructed, and started up the walk.

Just then the door flew open and the figure of a woman was outlined. Fred spoke to her briefly, and she hurried toward the car.

"Mrs. Gilfillan! I'm sure glad you're all right! Come in, all of you."

Leaning on Mrs. Cowperthwaite's arm, with Fred on the other side, Mrs. G. hobbled up the walk and into the house. Lissa trailed forlornly behind.

"See you tomorrow," Helen-Ann whispered, and began to run down the road toward her own house.

23

A telephone was ringing as they entered the house.

"Just make yourselves at home," Mrs. Cowperthwaite told them. "I'll be right back."

Lissa helped Mrs. G. to the sofa, propping her injured ankle on a pillow, with Oliver still in the pillowcase on her lap.

A mirror on the wall reflected a tall stranger with tangled blond hair and a soot-smudged face. Lissa looked at it curiously for a moment before she realized, with a sense of shock, that it was herself. She sank into a chair, her hand tight on Dewey's collar.

Just then Mrs. Cowperthwaite came back.

"That phone's been drivin' me crazy for the past hour," she said, regarding them kindly. "Well, now, it seems you folks could use a cup of coffee."

"It's good of you to take us in—" Mrs. G. began.

"For heaven's sakes, what're neighbors for! You do look plain tuckered. I'll get the coffee—it's all fixed—and then we'll see about beds."

She bustled off again, returning in a minute with a tray of steaming cups and a plate of homemade molasses cookies.

"There now—this'll pick us up a bit."

Lissa took a sip of the scalding brew, grasping the cup tight to still her shaking hands.

"My husband and the boys left a while back, when the first call came in. So we've got plenty of beds," Mrs. Cowperthwaite told them. Then she looked at Lissa.

"You must be Lissa. Jess's told me a lot about you."

"It's very g—good of you." Lissa was having a hard time keeping her voice under control.

"My, but you folks were lucky to get out." The warm concern in Mrs. Cowperthwaite's voice matched her ample, motherly-looking figure. "The worst part seems to be over your way, from what I hear."

She shook her head and clucked her tongue.

"This dry weather's been fierce, I'll tell you! Tom's been worried all month that a fire might start. And what with the woods full of campers this time of year, well. . . ." She shook her head again. "Did you walk all that way?"

"We ran, mostly," Lissa said.

"Where's your folks?"

Lissa told her about Nils and Barbara being in New York and Helen-Ann staying with her. She was too upset to notice the slight frown that crossed Mrs. Cowperthwaite's face.

"Well, this's a mighty poor introduction to the Pines for you, Lissa. But then I s'pose you might as well get used to it. Fire's a way o' life down here; isn't that right, Mrs. Gilfillan?"

"Yes, unfortunately."

Mrs. G. then told her about her accident, and how Lissa and Helen-Ann rescued her, coming by just in time. Mrs. Cowperthwaite nodded approvingly.

"First time's the worst," she said. "After a while, you kinda get so's you take it as a matter o' course."

She studied their wan faces.

"Here I am, goin' on, and what you both need is some rest."

She led Lissa upstairs to a bedroom.

"I'll fix Mrs. Gilfillan a bed on the sofa tonight. Now, honey, you just try and get some sleep. Everything'll be all right. Those men have been fightin' fire for years—they know what they're doin'. Don't you worry none now."

After she left, Lissa lay down on the bed, hugging her shoulders to try to stop their uncontrollable shaking. Her body ached with fatigue, but she couldn't sleep.

A kaleidoscope danced before her eyes—fragmented flashes of flame, cobwebby smoke wreaths, the faces of Helen-Ann and Mrs. G., the dark, echoing road, brooding unburned forest, sinuous curtains of fire again. . . .

For the first time during that endless night, she thought about the cabin—about her clothes, her books, all their possessions. Would they be gone? Barbara's beloved kiln, Nils' typewriter. . . .

She sat up in pure panic.

How would her parents feel, coming home to nothing but ashes!

They'd have no way to know about the fire. When they came home tomorrow, how would they find her?

Through gritty tearless eyes she looked at the clock on the dresser, its numerals glowing greenish in the dark. A quarter to five. In a few hours they'd be home.

Home.

But there wouldn't be a home to come to. . . .

Lissa woke to a gray morning.

Her eyes gradually focused on the unfamiliar room, and she lay in slowly mounting panic.

Where am I?

What happened?

Suddenly the memory of the past few hours flooded her. She threw back the quilt and leaped out of bed. The clock on the dresser said eight fifteen.

Running to the window, she looked out on the green branches of a sycamore tree. The sky was an ugly yellowish color, and the smell of smoke was bitter in the air. Several cars were parked in front of the house, but there was no sign of life anywhere.

Lissa opened the bedroom door and peered down the empty hall. From downstairs she heard a faint murmur of voices. Directly across she saw the bathroom door was open, so she crossed and went in. The stranger of last night stared back at her from the mirror above the sink.

Quickly Lissa washed and, finding a comb, drew it through her tousled hair. She noticed that her bedroom slippers had holes in the soles, and her blue bathrobe was gray with ash. Dried blood caked the two angry slashes on her arm where Oliver had scratched her. After she cleaned herself up as well as she could, she was reluctant to go downstairs, but there was nothing else to do.

The door to the living room was closed, so she went toward the kitchen. She could see Jess sitting at the table with two other men. A wave of embarrassment washed over her.

Jess leaped to his feet.

"Lissa! Come on in and have some breakfast."

Mrs. Cowperthwaite turned from the stove, smiling.

"Good mornin', Lissa. Sit down. I have griddle cakes comin'."

Jess pulled out a chair for her.

"Mom told me you were here. This's Ed Turner and Charley Sprague."

Lissa nodded and sat down.

"The fire's almost under control," Jess told her. "They got tractors in, over beyond your place, and plowed a line, and lit a backfire."

"An' the plane came over, just at daybreak," one of the men added.

"An airdrop," Jess explained to Lissa. "They fly over the fire, real low, and drop liquid fertilizer. It'll smother a head fire right off—"

"Lucky that old wind died down," Mrs. Cowperthwaite remarked, placing a heaping platter of pancakes on the table. "You fellas eat up now."

Lissa looked at the three of them, smoke-stained, with muddy boots and hollows of fatigue about their eyes.

"Our cabin," she faltered. "Is it. . . ."

Jess shook his head.

"I'm sorry, Lissa. I'm not sure—it's still too hot to get back in there, but . . . I'm afraid it might be gone. There's no way to tell for sure, of course, but they think the fire might've started somewhere near your place."

She nodded in silence.

"There's so many campers around," he went on, "but Dad's pretty sure they all got out safe, and yours is the only house back in there. So it really looks like no one was hurt. And they did save Mrs. G.'s house—got there in time to soak it down, so it didn't catch—"

"Oh, I'm glad for that!"

Lissa looked at Mrs. Cowperthwaite.

"Is Mrs. G. all right?"

"Sleepin' like a baby," Mrs. Cowperthwaite said with a smile. "Poor soul! She's too old to go traipsin' around, runnin' from fire. It's the Lord's blessin' you and Helen-Ann was there to help her."

Lissa pushed back her chair.

"I just don't know what—where—my folks don't know—"

Suddenly she was crying.

"Now, now—there, honey." Mrs. Cowperthwaite put a motherly arm about her shoulder. "You just go ahead an' have a good cry. Do you a world o' good. But don't you fret none—everything's going to be all right. . . ."

24

About an hour later Lissa was helping Mrs. Cowperthwaite to wash up the breakfast dishes. Jess and the men had gone out again, as there was one small patch still burning up the river a ways.

There was a soft knock on the kitchen door, and Helen-Ann came in. She was very pale, and her eyes were red-rimmed.

"I'm goin' to take Mrs. Gilfillan some breakfast now," Mrs. Cowperthwaite said, and left the kitchen.

Helen-Ann edged over to the sink.

"You okay?" she asked in a low voice.

"I guess so—how about you?"

"Yeah."

"Was your mother mad?"

"Oh, heck, no. But she was pretty scared. She'd sent my brother out to look for us, and she was sure glad to see me when I came in. Your folks back yet?"

"No. I guess they'd have no way of knowing—"

"Look, Lissa—I've got to talk to you, private like.

Is there somewhere we can go?"

"Let's go out on the back porch," Lissa said, sensing that something was terribly wrong.

Helen-Ann sat down on the porch step, lacing and unlacing her fingers nervously.

"It's about the fire," she began in a low voice. "I— oh, God! Lissa—I think maybe I might have started it."

Lissa stared at her anguished face in astonishment.

"I didn't mean to—honest! Oh, I just don't know—"

"But how—what do you mean?" Lissa felt her mouth go dry.

"That's the trouble—I just don't know for sure," Helen-Ann said miserably. "Remember, before I went to bed I drank that herb stuff, mixed in Coke?"

Lissa nodded. It seemed to have happened in another lifetime.

"Well, after I went to bed I began to feel pretty sick. I didn't want to wake you, so I went to the bathroom, an' I—I threw up."

"I never heard you. You should have called me."

"Well, I felt . . . ashamed, sort of, and I didn't want to bother you. I thought you'd think I was—pretty dumb, or something," Helen-Ann hesitated, and then went on, "I was still feelin' kinda funny, so I decided to go outside an' get some fresh air, an' so I sat under a tree for a while."

Lissa looked at her with sympathy.

"I smoked a cigarette—there was only one left in the pack—an' . . . oh, I'm *sure* I put it out. I threw the butt away, so's you wouldn't see it, an' then I came back in an' went to bed."

Helen-Ann was staring straight ahead, not looking at Lissa.

"I don't know how much later it was—I saw the fire through the window, an' that's when I came in to waken you."

Her face was somber.

"Oh, Lissa—what'll I do?"

Lissa was silent.

The night had been so frightful, so full of immediate danger, that she'd never given a thought to how the fire started. It simply was there, and had to be escaped.

Helen-Ann was openly crying now.

"Oh, please—please don't cry," Lissa said softly.

"It's all my fault," Helen-Ann sobbed.

Lissa put an arm about her shoulders.

"You don't know that for sure," Lissa comforted her. "It could have been anyone, or anything. Jess says that campfires—there're a lot of campers now—"

"If only I hadn't drunk that stuff an' got sick."

Lissa took a deep breath. There was something she had to say.

"Well then, it's—it's just as much my fault as yours. If I hadn't insisted that you drink it. . . ."

The words she didn't want to admit were spoken.

"What'll we do?" Helen-Ann implored.

All of Lissa's troubles paled before this inescapable thought.

"Should we tell someone?"

"I—I don't know. I guess we'll have to," Lissa hesitated. "Maybe—maybe we could tell Mrs. G. She'll know what's right to do."

Before Helen-Ann could reply, the kitchen door opened.

"Lissa," said Mrs. Cowperthwaite, "we're taking Mrs. Gilfillan home now. She wants you to come with her, to stay till your folks get back."

There was no chance to speak further with Helen-Ann, but as she left Lissa whispered to her, "Don't worry. I'll think of something."

25

A healing rain had begun to fall.

After thanking Mrs. Cowperthwaite for her kindness, Lissa and Mrs. G. once again climbed into Fred's old station wagon and were being driven back home.

Gazing in silence out the car window, Lissa only partly took in the ravaged land. Rain was pelting now, too late, and through the streaming glass she saw a blurred nightmarescape with steam writhing and coiling above it.

The underbrush was gone, and in places she could see far back into the forest. The taller trees, their trunks charred and fire-wrinkled, stood like basalt pillars in a ruined cathedral. Veils of smoke webbed their topmost branches.

"Well, here we be," Fred announced.

Mrs. G.'s house, like a smudge of charcoal, blended with the devastated forest around it. In silence they shuffled across the scorched lawn. As they rounded the porch they could see an ugly fire stain, blacker upon black, that blazed the back wall of the old house.

Fred let out a low whistle.

"That was a near un, missus."

It seemed years since Lissa'd been in that kitchen, instead of only last night. She helped Mrs. G. hobble to her rocking chair. Though pale, the old woman miraculously seemed to have recovered her spirits, just by being in her own home once more. Her gray eyes snapped with some of their customary sparkle.

"Lissa, you need some clothes."

Lissa looked down at her soiled blue bathrobe.

"You go upstairs and rummage in my cupboard. Help yourself to anything that'll fit."

She glanced at the old clock on the wall, ticking faithfully as if nothing had happened at all. Oliver, happy to be in familiar surroundings, vanished into some hidden corner of his own knowing, while Dewey padded upstairs behind Lissa. He had clearly decided that life was too much of a puzzle ever to be explained, but as long as Lissa was nearby, he was home.

When she appeared in the kitchen a little later, Lissa was wearing a lilac silk dress with ruffled cuffs, its hemline nearly reaching her ankles.

Mrs. G. chuckled.

"Why you look very stylish! Like a *Vogue* model. I knew if I lived long enough my clothes would come back in style again."

Lissa bravely tried to smile, without much success. She sat down on the high stool and clasped her hands tightly in her lap.

"Mrs. G.—I have to tell you something. And I don't quite know how."

"Why not begin at the beginning then?"

So, in fits and starts, making a wretched, disconnected story of it, Lissa told her the whole sorry tale. Mrs. G. listened without comment until she finished.

"And so it was really as much my fault as hers—I mean, I thought I was pretty cool, mixing up that infusion, and getting her to drink it, and all. . . ."

In the leaden silence that followed, Lissa waited. Fear, shame, and misery threatened to overcome her.

"Please put the kettle on. I think we need a cup of tea."

Without a word, Lissa got up. *I shouldn't be surprised,* she thought, as she filled the kettle in a kind of numb resignation. *Mrs. G. never says what you expect her to.* No word was spoken between them until they each held a steaming cup.

"When I first came to the Pine Barrens, nearly fifty years ago," Mrs. G. began, speaking slowly, thoughtfully, "it was, I thought, the beginning of a great adventure. My husband and I were young, with a small daughter. He'd just inherited a great deal of money, and buying and working the cranberry bogs was an exciting challenge."

Lissa wanted to cry out, But what has this got to do with me, with what I've just told you? It was not easy to hold her tongue. Coming to know Mrs. G. had taught her one valuable lesson at least—patience. So she kept quiet and listened.

"Oh, we were very grand then. We had great plans.

At first I was dismayed by the poverty and backwardness of the Pines people. I planned to build a school, to bring them books and culture, all of the things they were obviously lacking. But I soon learned that they didn't want what I was offering."

She paused, reflectively.

"They had their own ways, their own life. A good one for them, but I didn't know that then. And they shut me out. I learned loneliness, yes, and bitterness too. If they didn't need me, I thought, then I didn't need them either.

"And I made up my mind that my daughter would never have to endure what I was enduring. So I drove her away. Oh, not literally, of course. But I taught her to fend for herself, not to need anyone, not even me. And so, when she was grown, she left."

Mrs. G. was talking almost to herself now.

"When my husband died, and the money was gone, I couldn't leave. There was nowhere to go. Oh, I could have gone to my daughter, but we're both too proud for that. She had her own life by then."

She leaned forward and fixed Lissa with a piercing glance.

"That's when I finally learned to accept the Pine Barrens for what they are—both the place and the people," she said fiercely. "You cannot impose *yourself* upon a place. Especially the woods. You must come to them open, willing to accept them for what they are, and to accept what they have to give. But you never demand—you never say I will do, or I want. . . ."

She looked very old and tired, and there was a weariness in her voice.

"Do you understand anything of what I've been saying?"

Lissa, as she had listened, began to feel a faint stirring within herself. What the old woman was saying did begin to make sense, it did have some relation to what had just happened. And for the first time she began to see Mrs. G.'s own sense of estrangement and loneliness.

"Yes," she cried softly, suddenly, "yes, I think I do—or a part of it anyway."

She was silent for a moment.

"It really has got to do with love, hasn't it?"

Mrs. G. was looking at her with a strange expression, but Lissa didn't notice. Her thoughts came tumbling out.

"I mean, what you're really saying is that you've got to accept places, and people, for what they are . . . and love them for what they are, and keep yourself open to love. I was taking from the woods only what I thought I needed, without thinking of what I might give back.

"And when things change, or people change, why you've just got to accept that too."

Lissa stood up, spilling her tea in her excitement.

"That's what life is—change!" she cried in wonderment. "Nothing ever stays the same. Sometimes it's good and sometimes it's bad, but whatever, you've got to let yourself feel all of it. You can't be afraid to love, and you can't be afraid to let go again, if it's needed."

145

A faint smile crossed Mrs. G.'s face, and she nodded.

"I think we *both* have a great deal to think about," she said softly.

She put her teacup on the table.

"Now, to a more practical matter. As to how the fire started, I think there is much doubt. It is possible, of course, that it may have been Helen-Ann's cigarette, but again, it may have been something entirely different. That we will never know for sure.

"You know, there are sometimes as many as thirty fires a year throughout the Pine Barrens. A few are deliberately set, but most are accidental. I told you, fire happens here. It's something we have to live with.

"The main thing to remember always is that the woods are a trust. We've got to do everything in our power, personally, to see that fire never happens *because* of us. We who live here do have a great responsibility."

Lissa's gaze went to the window, and beyond it to the fire-ravaged trees.

"But—how can we repay—"

Mrs. G. followed her glance.

"You can never repay that," she said flatly. "But you've made the first installment—by facing up to it yourselves, by admitting that it could have been your own carelessness. You must explain that to Helen-Ann."

Just then they heard a car horn blare.

Lissa leaped to her feet and raced to the door. Nils and Barbara were running up the drive.

26

Lissa flung herself at Nils and felt his warm strong arms circle her, holding her close.

"Oh, Nils," she cried, "I'm so glad to see you!"

Tears glistened on his face.

"Ah, *min elskling!*"

Barbara was hugging her too, and they were all laughing and crying together.

"We heard about the fire on the news this morning," Barbara said. "We knew we couldn't phone you, and we were crazy with worry, so we just jumped in the car and drove like mad."

Her voice was shaky with relief, and she wiped away her tears on the sleeve of her shirt.

"Did you know your friend Jess was on national television? There were pictures of the fire fighters, and we recognized him," Nils said.

"That's when we really got scared," Barbara interrupted. "We knew then that the fire must be pretty close to home."

They had gathered in Mrs. G.'s kitchen, everyone talking at once.

"We came here first, because we told Lissa to come here in case of an emergency."

Nils' genial bearded face was more solemn than Lissa had ever seen it before as he took Mrs. G.'s hands in his own.

"When we left we had no idea there'd be any danger. How can we ever thank you?"

Mrs. G. returned the pressure of his hands. But there was a hint of steel in her gray eyes.

"It was *Lissa* who saved *me,*" she said quietly. "Mr. and Mrs. Evorssen, you have a fine daughter, a brave and loving girl. And you should be very proud of her. I think perhaps, that of all of us, she is really the most adult!"

Lissa felt almost light-headed. After all that had happened, the fear and exhaustion and relief, everything now seemed to have a dreamlike quality. All that she really understood was that she was safe, and with people who loved her, and it was good.

It was sometime later that Nils said, "I think maybe we ought to go over to the cabin and see if there's anything left."

Mrs. G. phoned the fire warden, who told her he thought that part of the woods had cooled enough because of the rain. If they were careful, they might go in. By now, the rain had fined to a drizzle, and a steamy fog clung everywhere like a shroud.

"You must come back and stay with me tonight," Mrs. G. called after them, "no matter what you find."

As the little red VW turned into their lane, Lissa saw how the tortured forest lay spent, a scarred cavern of silence.

At the side of the lane lay two small, charred furry bodies, squirrels unable to outrun the fire. Lissa looked away quickly. She had been concerned for Dewey and Oliver, but until this moment she had not given a thought to the wild creatures of the forest.

Squirrels and rabbits, possums and woodchucks, raccons, even the tiny wood mice and shrews—the woods teemed with shy life, glimpsed only occasionally. Now their secret rustlings were stilled.

Lissa mourned them in silence. Suddenly her own losses, no matter how great, seemed insignificant.

No one spoke as they drew up to the clearing where the cabin had stood. The stone fireplace loomed like a weary sentinel, guarding a pile of charred timber and rubble, all the ugly remnants of what had once been home.

Nils was the first to speak. He heaved a sigh and opened the car door.

"I guess we'd better poke around and see if we can salvage anything."

"Do we have to?" Barbara's face was stricken. "I'd just like to turn around, and never look back."

Nils put his arm around her shoulder.

"Lissa's safe," he said softly. "It could be a lot worse."

Barbara caught Lissa and hugged her tight.

"Oh, you're right, of course. I'm just being silly."

The next hour was one of the dreariest of Lissa's

whole life. She helped sift through the debris, salvaging bits and pieces of the past. Barbara's kiln was smoke-stained, but intact. Her wooden potter's wheel was burned beyond repair. Nils' typewriter had survived too, but the stereo set was only a twisted mass of melted wire and metal.

"Oh, look!" Barbara cried.

Triumphantly, she held up the blue spatterware coffeepot and hugged it to her breast.

Of her own things, Lissa found only her sewing machine, the case badly charred, and her silver-bangle bracelets and rings buried in the remains of her dresser. She gave only one dispirited glance to the soggy black rags that were all that was left of her clothes cupboard.

She felt a sympathetic hand on her shoulder.

"Come on, honey," Barbara whispered. "Let's forget about the rest of this mess. The first thing we've got to do is get you something to wear."

Lissa looked at her so woefully that Nils began to laugh.

"You look just like Jeanette MacDonald in that old movie about the San Francisco earthquake!"

In the long silk dress she'd borrowed and black rubber wading boots, Lissa felt unreal.

Suddenly she began to laugh, too.

Great whoops of wild, uncontrollable laughter swept all three of them—a vast healing release of tension. They clung to each other in the joy of simply being alive and together.

Nils finally wiped his eyes.

"Come on, you two nuts! Let's get out of here. We'll

drive over to Tuckerton and get Lissa some clothes, and then we'll go back to Mrs. G.'s. Later we can decide what to do next. . . ."

They climbed into the VW and drove down the lane without a backward glance.

DECEMBER

27

Lissa and Helen-Ann, their arms loaded with books, got off the school bus at Simpkins' Store. Cool feathery flakes of the season's first snow tickled their noses and melted in a moment as they hurried in to the apple-scented warmth. Lissa waved to Aunt Sally and began to gather things from the list Barbara had given her that morning.

"How're things comin' down to your new place?" Aunt Sally asked as Lissa piled her groceries on the counter.

"Pretty good," Lissa replied. "We've got four rooms done so far."

"Never thought anyone'd ever live in the old Jacob Leek place again," Aunt Sally remarked as she punched the cash register. "Why Lord! That old house must be goin' on two hunnerd years now—been empty since I was a girl."

Clearly, she thought the Evorssens were completely mad, but she was too polite to say so.

"We just love it," Lissa said. "My room looks right out on the river."

"You just gotta see it to believe it, Aunt Sally," Helen-Ann chimed in. "It's so pretty—what they've done with that old place. . . ."

They had rented the ancient and abandoned cedar-shingle house on the river, near the old church and graveyard at the end of town. Nils had gotten a part-time job at the boatbuilding plant in the next town down the river, so work on the house was progressing slowly. But Lissa and Barbara were learning how to use a hammer and saw, and the shabby old house was gradually becoming livable.

It was exciting, bringing it to life again. Lissa found a real joy in wondering whose feet had trod the splintered old floor-boards and about the generations of life that had once sheltered behind those ancient walls. She liked to imagine that some long-gone girl had leaned at the window that was now hers, watching plum-colored sunsets over the Pines and listening to the softly gleaming river lapping below.

It might not last forever—Nils hadn't promised that —but it would be hers for a while at least.

Helen-Ann was opening the ice-cream freezer.

"How about it, Lissa? Just one? I'll treat. I didn't eat any lunch today, honest."

"That's not the point," Lissa reminded her firmly. It's the calories . . ."

"I'll exercise a lot tonight." Helen-Ann was so apologetic that Lissa began to grin.

When Helen-Ann left, Lissa paid for her purchases

and started off down the road toward home. Huge starry flakes were falling straight and soundlessly from a windless sky, and already the road was filmed with white. Snow lay delicately along every branch and twig. Lissa breathed deep of the clean damp, savoring the reedy smell of the river.

"Hey, wait up!"

She turned to see Jess running after her.

"Your dad asked me to bring some finishing nails for him," he said, catching up with her.

Jess and his father were helping Nils with work on the old house.

Lissa lifted her face to the sky, feeling the moist, featherlight flakes brush her cheeks.

"Isn't this heavenly?" she breathed. "I wouldn't have believed snow could look so clean and beautiful!"

"Looks like this might be a good deep one," Jess observed, squinting at the clouds. "Dad has an old sleigh in the shed. If it gets deep enough, maybe we can borrow Fred Simpkins' horse and go for a sleigh ride."

28

By Saturday morning the snow was several inches deep. It crunched deliciously under Lissa's boots as she walked across Mrs. G.'s front yard. Dewey, following her, had poked his nose into every snowbank on the way. Now he had darted off in pursuit of a rabbit. He'd never catch it, but he always enjoyed the chase.

Everything was quilted with white, and under the snow the burned-out woods looked almost like any other winter woods. Right after the fire Jess had told her of the marvelous rejuvenating powers of the pine forest.

"You'll see, in spring," he's said. "It's fantastic how quick life comes back. The green starts and just spreads, almost as if the fire had nourished it."

Sparkling sunlight glanced and glittered from a brilliant sky, reflected from every surface until Lissa felt drunk-dazzled. Even Mrs. G.'s kitchen was bathed in this marvelous snow light, softened and filtered through the green plants at the window.

"Barbara sent you a loaf of cranberry bread," Lissa said as she stamped snow from her boots and hung her coat on a peg.

"How delightful!" Mrs. G. sniffed at the still-warm loaf. "We'll make a pot of tea and sample it."

As Lissa, without being told, took two rice-china cups from the shelf, she had a sudden flash of *déjà-vu,* that curious feeling of having done exactly the same thing in exactly the same way before.

Her mind flashed back to last summer, to the first time she visited this kitchen, frightened and lonely, and half believing the old woman was a witch. It seemed a whole lifetime ago.

"Lissa," Mrs. G.'s voice interrupted her thoughts, "I found something you might like to have."

Lissa took the old book handed to her—more of a pamphlet really—so fragile its brown edges crumbled lightly at her touch.

"It's an old almanac—1901," Mrs. G. said. "I found it in the back of a cupboard the other day It has some herbal recipes, and I thought you might like to have it."

The Gentlewoman's Herbal had been destroyed in the fire.

Lissa ran a thoughtful finger over the brittle paper cover.

"Thank you," she said slowly, and met Mrs. G.'s eyes, "but I think I'm through with all that now."

"But surely you're not going to give up making your herbal bath salts. Your friend Marcy liked them, and I'm sure some the local antique and gift shops would buy them."

"Oh . . . well, maybe later. When Barbara gets her pottery going again."

Lissa perched on the high stool.

"You know, I think I really made them because of Marcy—because I thought she'd like them, and to sort of, well . . . hang onto her. And now . . . Marcy has her own life. Oh, we're still good friends, of course. I think we always will be. But I've got a new life, too, now—my own, here in the Pine Barrens."

Mrs. G. seemed about to speak, but Lissa hurried on.

"Oh, I know it won't last forever. I can't expect that Nils will ever stay in one place very long. It's the way he is. I know that now. And wherever he goes, Barbara and I will go too. We're a family, and we'll stick together."

Lissa smiled warmly at Mrs. G. It was an older-than-thirteen smile.

"But I do know something else now, too—for absolute *sure*. I've found it, the place where I belong. No matter where I go from now on, the Pine Barrens is *home*. It's my place—I belong here. I can't explain why, exactly, but it's something I just know. And I'll *always* come back."

Lissa stretched her long legs and stirred her tea.

"And anyway, we've got a whole year—Nils promised that. . . ."